Acclaim for
Out of Mercy

"A savage, horrifying and gut-bustingly funny Western, set in an Old West that would have made John Wayne turn and run for his life and featuring a cast of characters so richly imagined I'm afraid they'll turn up in my nightmares. I loved every word of it."

—Scott Phillips, *New York Times* bestselling author of *The Ice Harvest*

"Think Elmore Leonard or Cormac McCarthy—with a dash of Nick Hornby to keep things suitably bent. But make no mistake—Ashley has a strong, savage, uncompromising voice of his own. *Out of Mercy* is the kind of flat-out, heart-stopping, psycho-emotional thrill ride that just might put this author on the map with the giants. Personally, I can't wait to read more of Jonathan Ashley's work—once I recover from this one."

—Jerry Stahl, *New York Times* bestselling author of *Permanent Midnight*

"Hard, stark and brilliant, *Out of Mercy* is the best Western I've read in years."

—Benjamin Whitmer, author of *Cry Father*

"A dark gem, a bleak tale of survival and revenge in the bloody hills of Kentucky. Vividly written, filled with compelling characters and laced with black humor, this is frontier noir at its best."

—James Reasoner, author of *Texas Wind*

OUT OF
MERCY

ALSO BY JONATHAN ASHLEY

Jon Catlett Series
The Cost of Doing Business
South of Cincinnati
The Last Fallout (*)

Stand Alones
Friends in Low Places (*)
Out of Mercy

(*) – coming soon

JONATHAN ASHLEY

OUT OF MERCY

Down & Out Books
3959 Van Dyke Rd, Ste. 265
Lutz, FL 33558
www.DownAndOutBooks.com

Cover design by JT Lindroos

ISBN: 1-948235-03-X
ISBN-13: 978-1-948235-03-7

For my father,
Franklin D. Ashley

PART ONE

What the Apaches Left Her

1

The bartender in the over-starched shirt talked too much for his own good. Without so much as a glance in the woman's direction, he passed her in his hurry to refill the blacksmith's bourbon and the steamboat captain's empty gin tumbler. Both men wore frozen grins, feigning over the bartender's ribald tales of drifters and drummers cuckolding the wives of local entrepreneurs.

She was the only woman in the saloon, and the names that poured from the bartender's lips meant nothing to her. She had no frame of reference, as she, herself, was an outsider in this sliver of a tavern, crammed into a mountain face of West Virginia. The room had no windows, and the space around the batwing doors was the only source of light. These kinds of men didn't mind the dark. They preferred not to look too closely at one another. They were not seeking companionship or camaraderie. They'd come here so they wouldn't have to be alone in their isolation. What they wanted was the simplicity of the suffocating silence, if only for a few hours.

A faint smell of urine pervaded the air. Someone had mistaken a corner of the room for an outhouse, presumably several hours earlier, and the bartender had either neglected to or didn't feel the need to clean up the mess.

So I'm not the only thing being ignored around here, she thought with a grin. *No better than stale piss.*

While she wore beggar's clothing, she knew that wasn't the reason for the bartender's disinterest. Neither was it her boots with the soles coming loose or her torn and tattered suit coat. She knew, too, that her sex wasn't the issue. Certain types of women drank freely in bars from West Texas to West Virginia, to nary a raised eyebrow.

It was the exotic markings on her face, too thick to hide with even the most expensive stolen makeup, that gave her away as goods damaged by native hands. Her high cheekbones, her pursed lips and hourglass figure, none of that would allow a white man to overlook where she had been. Taking her hand would be half a step above marrying a Negro, if that.

She examined the dirt under her nails, stood, reached over the bar, palmed a shot glass, flipped it over and, eyes on the negligent bartender, brought its bottom back down onto the mahogany surface. A lightning bolt shot up her arm as the sharp *crack!* reached the ear of the bartender, who satisfied her with an overly demonstrative flinch. The blacksmith and the captain winced likewise. All conversation came to an abrupt halt. As if to emphasize the point, she continued to tap the glass on the bar in a slow, deadly rhythm.

At first, the bartender only stared at her impassively. She shrugged and continued her tapping. She had waited out tougher cases.

The bartender's hand shot out, catching her on the wrist mid-stroke. She broke a half-smile.

"Is there something I can do for ye?"

She shook his grip loose and placed the glass lightly upon the bar, tipping her head to the bourbon on the bottom shelf.

He sighed and shook his head as if a drink for a customer, especially a dirty girl in a derby hat with scars under her eyes, was decidedly not worth the interruption of one of his stories.

"Why didn't ye jest holler? What's a matter? Cat got yer tongue?"

She stepped back from the bar, opened her mouth, and with all the force she could muster pushed what little tongue the Apaches had left her out for the audience to see. The stub had been stitched badly, leaving blots of flesh so red they gave the appearance of fresh blood.

The blacksmith's face drained of all color and he looked away, eying the high ceiling corners while he fiddled with his glass.

The captain rose, reached inside his coat, and placed a few coins on the bartop, shuffling briskly toward the double doors.

"I'll be seeing ye boys after my next run upriver."

The bartender opened his mouth, then quickly shut it, nodding. His brow furrowed deeper as he picked up the shot glass and turned to the bourbon.

The mute took her seat, glad she had run off the captain and not the blacksmith, as he was her target. She'd been left with specific instructions. If the Yankee blacksmith got on his horse to head home from the tavern, she was to follow him and render him unconscious, but unconscious only.

While none of them, the mute in particular, had any problem with killing, the law arrived a lot faster when bodies were involved.

* * *

Half a mile east, near the edge of a steep, tree-lined cut of mountain, her partners ascended to the second floor of the blacksmith's humble abode.

From the outside, the home did appear modest, an un-painted, two-story wooden structure with a thatched roof. But the façade was merely a trick, no doubt to dissuade brigands like themselves. In stark contrast to what one saw from the dirt road, the inside looked like a palace, an offense to the starving, a gaudy temple of greed and decadence adorned with opulent antiques and artwork. Fortunately, the blacksmith had a mouth when away from home, spread-ing word in Virginia of his wartime spoils that allowed him to live like a king among the rabble poor and homeless.

So while the blacksmith slid his glass across the bar for another shot of bourbon, Tompal Banks feasted his eyes upon the stacks of crates in the attic of the blacksmith's house, six in all, lined up like coffins after the gallows, the only other fixtures in the space being a broken mirror and a chest of drawers laid on its back.

Cody Williams approached the first two stacks. He turned and smiled into the broken mirror, a crescent moon forming across the scarred, dark night of his face. Having to lean down to see his reflection, with pure muscle poking out of the flannel of his shirt, the barrel-chested man of six-foot-three ran his hands through his curly white hair then stood upright, shifting his attention back to the business at hand.

He slid the lids off the top two crates simultaneously.

Tompal removed his hat in reverence.

He knew a man up near Falls City that could make use

of a few of these crates, a bet-taker and whoremaster who could arm a few of his lieutenants well with this lot and make a profit with the surplus firepower. Tompal would sell low. It was not as if he had much overhead.

They worked quickly, setting each crate side by side, opening and examining the contents.

There were Schofields, Rogers & Spencer revolvers, Remington Rolling Block single shots, Sharps buffalo rifles, and plenty of ammunition for each.

"Some of these fine pieces of hardware were just issued in the last few years," Cody said. "I think our man may have himself a little side business, Tompal, and I believe this may be his inventory we're lookin' at."

"You think he's selling these things?" Tompal couldn't move his eyes from the crates.

"These ones are still here so they obviously ain't sold yet."

"I appreciate that observation, Cody."

"Though, I do think he may be intending to sell them."

"An inventory?"

"Could be. What would he need with so many of the same model? That's what gets me. A lot of parties would like to get their hands on what's in these-here crates."

"Well, Cody." Tompal laughed. "Our businessman is about to suffer a loss."

Tompal chose a revolver and a rifle for himself, holding it to his chest as a soldier in formation.

He would discard his worn-out Winchester on the trail back to town.

2

If another patron came in and tried to chat her up, the others now knew of her condition and could enlighten the irritant. Tompal had often assured the mute that her condition made for an easy retreat, an unending excuse for ignoring the attempts some asshole would inevitably make at polite conversation.

She heard the batwing doors squeak followed by the sound of scraping boots, and turned to see two bearded men dressed in leather jackets, black denim, and hats of the same shade. Their faces were darkened with dirt and their bootheels worn to stubs.

Probably miners, she thought.

They stood and examined their surroundings for a moment until the bartender interrupted the silence.

"Jessup, Cal."

The one on the right spat on the sawdust floor and ignored the welcome. The other removed his hat and said, "A bottle."

Finally, a man of few words, the mute thought sourly.

The one who had yet to speak had taken notice of the mute, running his eyes up and down her figure, probably

6

guessing her age, *hoping for younger,* she thought by the looks of him.

She had dealt with their type.

The quiet man stepped between the mute and the blacksmith. He grinned as he removed her hat and set it on the bar. The last man to touch her hat now resided in a graveyard somewhere just outside of Richmond. But she couldn't react yet. She'd promised Tompal to avoid making any more of a scene than her mere presence called for.

The bartender placed an unopened bottle of bourbon in front of the quiet man. Eyes on the mute, he unscrewed the lid, tossed it over his shoulder, and drank straight from the lip.

She felt hot air on her neck, an odor so foul it dominated the stench of old urine from the corner. Had she not been immune to the harsh exhales of unclean men she might have vomited all over the mahogany. She turned toward the source, the breath of a feral beast picking up the scent of a female in heat.

"Throw me them keys to that guest room ye got upstairs," the talker said to the bartender without taking his eyes off the mute.

The bartender shook his head again, this time with less ego, more dreadful premonition.

"Cal..." the bartender began.

Cal shot the bartender a quick, cold glance. "Keys." His gaze returned to the mute.

The bartender nodded and reached under the bar, coming up with a single brass key, which he sat in front of the mute. Cal placed his hand over the key and shot a look at his companion.

The mute glanced back and forth between the blacksmith

and the bartender—both refused to meet her eyes, knowing and doing nothing to stop the imminent violation the two dirty, leather-clad galoots were intending to commit.

Cowards, she thought.

It didn't matter. She was used to handling these kinds of things herself.

"Let's go," the one to her right, the quiet man Jessup, finally spoke. "I'm pretty sure from the looks of ye, darlin' that ye know the routine."

"She ain't no stranger to any of this," Cal said. "And for good reason. Give her a bath, maybe let her hair grow out a little, put some garters and a dress on her and she'd be a brick shithouse, pardner."

"I kind of like her hair short."

"When we get them clothes off I'm betting she's built like a goddamn Winchester."

"I don't think there's much to be done about these." Cal snaked his thumb along one of the three blue tattoo lines under her left eye that ran all the way down her cheeks, extending to her jaw.

"Where'd ye get them, girl? Ye got some native in ye?" Jessup asked.

"She can't speak," the bartender offered.

"So she's all fucked up," Jessup crowed.

Jessup grabbed her coat and yanked. She went with it, standing at attention and waiting for his next direction.

"Up them stairs."

He pushed her on.

The bartender stared at the door beyond the rotted, wooden banister up the stairs. Perhaps two minutes had passed since they'd goaded her along to her fate, locking the door behind them.

A shriek sounded from behind the guest-room door, followed by the sound of something heavy hitting the floor above, shaking free ancient dust from the wood slats overhead.

The bartender stood, reaching under the mahogany and coming up with a Schofield. The blacksmith stepped back from the bar, edged toward the far end of the saloon, and crouched.

The door opened and the mute stepped out, a Bowie knife in hand, a clown's smile painted in blood across her lips.

Jessup appeared in the half-dark of the doorway behind her, his haggard face bloody and covered in sawdust. The mute, noticing the bartender glancing over her shoulder, turned just as Jessup raised the Colt revolver. She grabbed his wrist and diverted the pistol's aim, bringing the Bowie knife up to strike. Jessup stopped her, clutching her wrist.

They began to move in a circle, two figures entangled in a ghastly dance, waltzing quickly toward the banister.

With Jessup's back to the railing, the mute flung her weight against him. The barrier gave way. They landed on the bar, the mute on top, neither letting go of the other's wrist, their grips on weapons fixed to kill.

The bartender dropped his gun and backed up to the mirrored liquor shelf, impotent against the violence before him.

With one hand, the mute forced Jessup's fist against the mahogany bar. With the other she slowly raised the blade against the pull of his hand.

"Cunty little bitch, ain't ye?" a voice called from somewhere above.

Upstairs, beyond the broken banister from where the drained words had drifted, there stood Cal, clutching his britches to his crotch, blood seeping through the cracks between his fingers.

He lifted his other arm, revealing a sawed-off double-barrel fitted with pistol grips.

"Ye get off him right now and face yer fate like the cock-sucker our Lord and Savior meant ye to be," Cal ordered.

The mute shrugged and turned back to Jessup, raising the knife higher, taking a chance that Cal's threat was an empty one, that at least there was honor among scoundrels. The scatter of the buckshot would hit his partner, as well.

Keeping his pistol at bay, Jessup opened his mouth, threw his head back and sank his teeth into her wrist. She held on for a moment longer then collapsed off the bar onto her knees, dropping the Bowie knife and grasping the bleeding bite mark. Jessup rolled off the bar and stood over her.

He thumbed back the hammer.

Then, taking notice of Tompal and Cody filling the doorway, pump rifles held loosely at their sides, Jessup hesitated.

Cody stared at Jessup, his eyes untiring.

"What the fuck are ye looking at?" Jessup shouted, addressing Tompal and avoiding the hard gaze of the white-haired black man at his side.

"We lookin' for a friend a' ours," Tompal said.

"Do I look like the goddamned good Samaritan to you?" Jessup took another step toward the mute. "Yer business is yers and mine is mine, nigger lover. That love thy neighbor, turn the other cheek horse shit'll get ye killed around these parts. Now I have business to attend to if ye don't mind." Jessup nodded toward the kneeling mute.

"That's our friend right there." Tompal nodded toward the mute. "So you could say we mind."

"And," Cody followed, "you could also say it's our business."

"The nigger speaks." Jessup spat toward Cody, but continued to address Tompal. "Can he dance too?" And the man who just seconds before had found himself on the losing end of a two-to-one botched attempted violation of a mute girl shuffled his feet back and forth, flailing his empty hand in the air next to his head.

Tompal chuckled. "Cody, that look like dancing to you?"

Cody laughed, unsmiling and a little too loudly, no doubt for Jessup's benefit. "Maybe at the row of outhouses when all the doors are locked." He cocked his head to one side, favoring Jessup with a humorless grin. "You do know what 'no vacancy' means, don't you, big man?"

Jessup halted his shuffle mid-step. Eyes blazing, he put a boot to the mute's back and pressed the barrel of his pistol to her head.

Tompal pumped a round into his Colt and leveled the shotgun at Jessup.

Cal stumbled toward the banister and raised the sawed-off, but froze when he saw Cody had already taken aim at him.

"I don't think your partner up there wants to die with his pants down," Tompal said. "Y'all don't want the whole town knowing what she done to him, do you?"

"She ain't walking away from this," Jessup sneered.

"What do you propose?" Tompal replied, gently, as if

asking a lover whether she preferred to go upstairs or receive a gentleman's walk home.

"I propose ye strut the fuck out of here before we handle ye in a similar fashion." Jessup turned the gun on Cody. "Then maybe for good measure we'll string your smart-mouthed nigger here up a tree."

"Your choice." Tompal closed an eye and took aim.

"You're goddamn right it's my choice," Jessup yelled. "Who you think ye are walkin' in here all—"

It was Jessup's last word before Tompal shot him between the eyes.

Cody fired twice. Splinters from the banister exploded in the smoke as Cal spun around, toppled off the second level, and landed facedown on the sawdust barroom floor.

Cal groaned. Tompal took two paces toward the stairs and got a bead on the downed man to take his second shot of the afternoon. An arterial spray rose from the other side of Cal's head and all signs of life ceased.

The mute stood, brushing herself off as Cody and Tompal approached.

"You all right, sister?" Cody placed an arm around her shoulders.

"Nothing she couldn't handle." Tompal lifted his black Stetson to his head from where it rested by a leather cord around his neck, glanced over his shoulder at the bartender, and extended a hand.

"Kindly hand me the lady's hat?"

The bartender shivered behind the mahogany, tears welling in his eyes as he took in the massacre the stone-faced Negro and the white man had created within a matter of seconds.

"Could you make some haste, mister?" Tompal said.

"I'm fuckin' aging here."

The blacksmith, standing at the far end of the bar, eyed the men and their guns, rich men's rifles that did not match the rags they wore.

The bartender carefully handed over the derby, crumpled from where Jessup had landed on it. "What's she doing?" Tompal turned to see the mute leaning over Jessup, a handful of his stringy, oily hair in one hand, her Bowie knife in the other, working its blade along his scalp.

"I told you we ain't got time for that, baby child." Cody approached the kneeling mute. He hooked a big hand under her arm and pulled her to her feet, but not before she got a good yank on Jessup's hair, tearing a dollar-bill-sized portion of his scalp free of his skull.

She held it over her head for the survivors to see, allowing it to bleed down onto her face, down the opening of her flannel shirt, under which upstairs, Cal had reached down to fondle her while he was in her mouth, before she bit down, before she had reached to the small of her back and unsheathed the knife, bludgeoning Jessup with its handle as Cal wailed, paralyzed, drooling on the mattress, cradling his loins.

She offered the fresh scalp to Tompal, who waved it away.

"You take it. It's good as yours anyway."

The bartender's knees hit the floor. He vomited into a mop bucket behind the bar.

The three tramped across the muddy thoroughfare. The crowd that had gathered cleared a path.

They came to the hitching post in front of the hardware

store. Tompal and Cody sheathed their rifles, and while Tompal undid the wagon from the post, Cody spoke to the two mules in hushed tones. Mounting her mare, the mute reached under her saddle and brought out a string of dried scalps, making a great show of attaching her latest trophy before draping it around the horse's neck for the pleasure of the gawking, hushed crowd.

Tompal hoisted himself onto the left side of the riding plank and reached for the reins. Cody tossed them up to Tompal and positioned himself between the heads of the two mules, his hands on their muzzles, as if in prayer. Tompal cleared his throat. Cody placed an ear near the mouth of the mule on the left, then the mule on the right, gave them one final pat, rounded to the wagon, and hoisted himself up. Tompal handed him the reins. "You know if I was driving, we'd have seen the backside of this town by now."

Cody huffed. "If you were driving, we'd still be halfway between here and Charleston."

"What's it you say to them?"

"Never you mind." Cody eased the mules out onto the rut-riddled street. The wagon, worse for the wear, groaned while the still-stunned throngs parted to allow them through.

"Stop right there!" In front of the saloon steps stood the blacksmith, holding Jessup's revolver at aim with both hands. His eyes shifted between them and the wagon.

A rotund man with a gray mustache dressed in thick flannel and faded jeans stepped out from the crowd, a crudely minted tin sheriff's star pinned to his shirt.

"What's going on here, Nate?" the sheriff asked the blacksmith.

"These three killed two men inside, Sheriff," Nate's voice cracked with every other syllable. "They also stole from me."

The sheriff examined Tompal and Cody lazily, as if he had better things to do. "What was it they stole?"

"Look in their wagon," Nate the blacksmith puffed. Regaining his confidence, he twitched the gun barrel toward the wagon.

"You mind?" the Sheriff asked Tompal.

"You goddamned right I mind," Tompal said, pointing at Nate. "That man's a lunatic and this-here's my private property. I got constitutional rights. I got the right to pass through this territory unmolested by the likes of you shameless sodomites. So you—" Tompal pointed to the sheriff now, "—don't be getting no funny ideas. You keep that cock of yours in your britches where it belongs."

"Calm down, mister," the sheriff said.

"I'm a United States citizen and I insist on being treated like one."

"Tanner." For the first time Nate addressed the sheriff by name.

Tompal recorded the glance between the lawman and the blacksmith and understood that Cody had been right. The stolen guns were an inventory and the local sheriff was being paid a duty by this arms dealer for extra muscle when the occasion called for it.

The sheriff heaved a sigh as he undid the flap on his holster.

Tompal reached to the small of his back and drew the pistol.

The sheriff was starting to speak again when Tompal fired into his open mouth, a splattering of red covering several of the townspeople behind. Screams and prayers for deliverance rose from the crowd as they dispersed in all directions, save that blocked by Tompal's ragged little army.

The mute emerged from behind the wagon with Bowie knife drawn and twirled it through the air, the blade catching the blacksmith in the neck as Cody shot him through the cheek.

"So much for leaving no bodies in our wake," Tompal said, a lilt in his voice. "Every damn town's the same."

3

This was the fall of 1882.

After killing four men in West Virginia, the mute, Cody Williams, and Tompal Banks, killer of twenty-three by his own estimates, crossed the Ohio River under the remnant lights of dusk.

They camped just beyond the state line, still in the mountains. The biting October winds knocked free dead and dying leaves from the oaks and pines that provided meager shelter. Nature had afforded them room for only one to sleep in moderate comfort in the wagon amidst the crates. They offered the space to the mute.

She gave no response and did not move. She would suffer the elements with them.

Cody tended to the mute's wound, the bite Jessup had delivered, pouring whiskey he'd taken from the saloon into the already-scabbing teeth marks and wrapping the wound with tearing from a feed sack. With her free hand, the mute squeezed the last drops of blood from the souvenir she'd ripped from Jessup's crown over the other scalps to feed their long journey into the afterlife.

Tompal made a fire to cook the squirrels he'd shot for

their supper. His blue eyes shone in the moonlight, harder than the stone walls and steel bars he'd avoided since his bitter youth.

While the air filled with the syrupy scent of the cook fire, Tompal swore that they would not kill anyone in this land new to all of them, this place called Kentucky.

It was a vow they would break before the next sunset in the town of Mercy, where their trek to Falls City would come to a staggering halt.

PART TWO

Mercy

4

"When you see the abomination that causes desolation standing where it does not belong, let the reader understand..."

Reverend Thurman recited apocalyptic gospel from memory. He sweated profusely. His thin white hair jutted out in all directions as he stood before his congregation with hands in a stop-motion gesture. He appeared as if lifting some invisible weight toward the canvas canopy above.

Metal stakes held down the sadly drooping sides and the ends were securely tied to cypress trees. When Thurman first set up the tent, he christened his new church Riverside Redeemer, painting the name boldly in black on the canvas wall facing the river for the benefit of travelers and the sinful crews of steamboats.

Before he was even halfway warmed up, Thurman had already met eyes with every member of his congregation: these, the great unwashed the savior had walked among who could only find pride and salvation with like souls. Unlike Father Garrison at Holy Innocents, the half-pagan excuse for a place of worship, Thurman did not speak from a podium, favoring the methods and mannerisms of the street preachers and snake charmers who had so inspired him during his wartime travels. These were men of God who stood close to their people when they felt the Holy Spirit move them, sharing the current of salvation. They were the same men who had salvaged Thurman from the drinking and whoring that sent many a fellow Confederate veteran to an early grave and to the eternal damnation awaiting beyond.

The population of Mercy was predominantly of Scotch-Irish and German ilk. Around two thirds were Catholic and the rest Presbyterian. They had left their mother countries to escape the potato famine and oppressive government, European peasants tired of having to eat raw birds in winter to keep from starving.

Thurman made short work of the Catholics who, in his view, had for the most part, attended their religion's services out of familial tradition and habit with no real faith. All he'd had to do was give them a small taste of his showmanship. Compared to the countless mind-numbing Latin masses they'd sat through, the reverend looked like God himself. The Catholics were not alone in their decline. Our Mother of Sorrows, Mercy's Presbyterian Church on Ninth Street, had lost over a third of its regular attendees to Thurman's Baptist preaching.

Many of Thurman's converts were drifters, men and women scattered by the aftermath of the war. Some had found jobs at the pig-iron factory and needed Thurman to help quench their resentment at the drudgery, the long hours, and declining wages. Others were steamboat workers who spent two weeks on the river followed by two weeks drinking and whoring the shantytowns that lay on its banks.

Abe Tremont had suffered the consequences of such a

lifestyle. He had come to Thurman drunk and weeping with a confession. He'd woken from a blackout in a shotgun shack on Frenchman's Row, a vice-ridden shantytown on the outskirts of Louisville, soaked in the blood of the teenage Negress who lay butchered on the mattress beside him.

Thurman had baptized Tremont the very next day, his congregation marching in formation to the river where the boatman was immersed and thus reborn.

"...Then let those who are in Judea flee to the mountains. Let no one on the roof of his house go down or enter the house to take anything out."

He had also converted the now defunct Mills gang who, despite their reformation, lived in self-imposed exile save Sundays on a farm out on Seven Mile Lane. During their exploits they had been led by Ike Mills and his drooling father, Erastus, whose right half had been paralyzed by a stroke he suffered while raping a retarded thirteen-year-old girl in Knoxville. The old man attributed the stroke as God's punishment for a life lived in the most godforsaken depths of sin.

The gang stole cattle and marauded the surrounding counties in the immediate years following their return from the war. Then they turned to robbing, torturing, and sodomizing passing Union officials traveling south from Ohio and Illinois to assist in the Reconstruction. It had been revealed more than once to Reverend Thurman that the sexual violations had often taken place after the Union men had been killed in some torturous hell.

Cases were never made against the Mills gang for lack of witnesses and evidence, but everybody knew about them. The town of Mercy lived in fear, especially those residents who had fought for the North. While the Mills' never subjected the town itself to their wickedness, it was believed there would come a day when that courtesy expired.

The day never arrived.

Thurman succeeded in stopping the gang's savagery, employing the gospel where the laws of man had failed. For this the mayor and city council allowed him his madness, never once siccing Marshal Don Hayes and his deputies on the reverend when he besieged out-of-towners on the street with his particular brand of evangelism.

"Let no one in the field go back to get his cloak. How dreadful it will be in those days for pregnant women and nursing mothers!"

At this particularly gruesome verse, Thurman shifted his eyes to Milton Skinner, a deacon at Holy Innocents who more often than not attended the tent services wearing thick-lensed spectacles and a fake beard. Only Thurman was aware of his true identity.

Skinner had confided in the reverend over the exceedingly liberal Father Garrison who he believed was going to be the damnation of the entire state. It had been reported to him by a good Catholic that during confession the priest had begun downplaying the importance of the immortal soul, urging his parishioners to help other people rather than indulge in shame and self-flagellation. Instead of assigning an "Our Father" when someone confessed a sin, Garrison would instead suggest the parishioner make a trip to the Veterans Hospital in Louisville for a weekend to volunteer or that they invite a beggar into their home to feed and bathe the poor soul.

The sad part was that the priest was having some sway.

Many saw sense in the idea that helping others would

trump acts more conducive to the salvation of their own souls such as the repetition of the "Hail Mary" or donating Bibles to be sent to missionaries in the newly formed western territories.

The deacon was at a loss.

Skinner, despite his loyalty to the Pope, was more loyal to Christ and had begun to see things from Thurman's point of view. Brother had already been set against brother, a sure sign the Second Coming was imminent. Preparations needed to be made. God's chosen representatives would surely be held accountable on that Day of Judgment for those remaining unrepentant. He also understood the importance of holy justice. In his view, the only way to prove to the Lord's flock that his word was true was to protect them from the war's damaged goods that drifted into the state from Tennessee and the Virginias seeking to destroy Mercy's efforts at peace and prosperity. These types were most dangerous because of their haunting histories, experience that granted them the parlous ability to lead astray these converts' newly found and fragile faith.

Thurman sprinted through the crowd to Will Chiles, the father of Margaret, found raped and decapitated a little over a year ago on the banks of the Ohio.

Thurman, then with no congregation, had been preaching at any passerby unfortunate enough to encounter the reverend. When the killer was apprehended, Thurman stood outside the jail and then, during the trial, on the courthouse steps, quoting Old Testament scripture, demanding a prompt hanging.

The murderer, Raymond Earl Duncan, was found passed out drunk in the alley between Schultze's Boarding House and the Arcade with Margaret's head in his lap.

The trial took so long because Duncan, a drifter and a drunkard from Arkansas, had suffered war injuries that left his right arm useless. The cut that severed Margaret's head had started on the left side of her neck, meaning the assailant had likely used his right hand. This gave the defense some short-lived leverage. Talk of planted evidence and a killer still on the loose did not dissuade the jury, even though a patient judge had allowed the defense numerous extensions to contact and secure the testimonies of several so-called experts on postmortem examination.

Then the prosecution brought in the children Duncan had exposed himself to and the defendant was as good as dead.

The lengthy trial was the end of that particular judge's career in Mercy.

The one with the cloven foot had won that battle, Thurman would preach, instilling fear in the citizenry, distrust in the workings of the law inspired by God Himself.

Thurman took the opportunity to minister. He spent hours at the bedside of Will Chiles, a month-long suicide watch. Chiles' wife had succumbed to TB two years after Margaret's birth. With his daughter's murder, he had lost everything. A year later he had Jesus Christ and His disciple, Reverend Thurman, as his spiritual leader in Mercy.

Thurman stepped next to Will Chiles, now ruddy and standing straight, faithful that his daughter had died a virgin, save the rape, which Thurman assured him did not count.

Chiles took Thurman into a deep embrace.

Tears streamed down the reverend's cheeks, over the red ulcers that had grown worse every year since his return from the war, now almost overtaking his face.

"Pray that this will not take place in winter because those will be days of distress unequaled from the beginning when God created the world, until now and never to be equaled again."

5

Don Hayes awoke in an eight-by-ten cell, one of two in the small jail, the farthest from the door. The chill in the hollow place was unpleasant. It came from the cold outside, seeping through the dank sepulchral stone that of which the cell's walls had been constructed. He leaned up on his elbows and then squatted, rubbing at his eyes with both hands, checking his mustache for snot and the bristles on his chin for saliva. Sharp pain traveled the axis of his skull when he attempted to stretch his neck.

He felt like he had been hit upside the head by one of the drunken ironworkers he often had to arrest. But the only blows he had withstood recently were courtesy of John Barleycorn and Hayes was always the instigator and loser in such quarrels.

He usually ached in the mornings, hung over or not, years of hard living finally taking their toll on him. This particular sunrise was worse than most. Every year when the weather started to turn his drinking grew worse. Maybe it was because every great loss he'd suffered occurred when the leaves were falling.

Hayes watched his father fall drunk from the roof of his

childhood home where the old man had been repairing a leak. He landed on his head, stood, said "Goddammit," and dropped dead into a pile of raked leaves. Hayes had killed his first Yankee soldier, crawling on autumn leaves to slit the throat of the sleeping private.

And the loss that had exiled him from the cold bed in his empty house to the prison cell where he slept most nights had occurred in the month of October under skeletal branches.

It was not his favorite time of year.

As his eyes adjusted to the sunlight coming through the steel bars, he wished there was a woman in his life who loved him just enough to have coffee brewing, ready for him in the morning.

Surely he was still worth that much.

He slowly tucked the brown hair he'd allowed to grow too long behind his ears. Like a child who'd burnt himself on a steam pot, he was wary of moving his head any more than he had to. He stood and plodded through the open cell door, relieved at the silence of the empty jail. He glanced at the clock above the gun rack on the far wall across from the cells.

That bastard Scoggins was late again and Masterson had left early.

He certainly hoped they weren't at church, at least not the one under the canvas of that crazy son of a bitch Thurman. The last thing he needed was to have his only two deputies in the pocket of a lunatic.

Hayes himself had fallen behind in attendance at Holy Innocents, the Catholic church on Lexington Avenue his wife had dragged him to every Sunday.

Perhaps bachelorhood did have its perks.

He would have to remember, if he ever ran into him, to thank the drummer that laid her on a haystack then swept her off to Arkansas. She sent a handful of letters detailing the matrimonial crimes he had been guilty of, blaming him for her infidelity.

Hayes had borne witness to one of the many haystack romps, months before her departure. He'd passed out drunk in his stable and woken to the sounds, never alerting them to his presence as he watched the drummer defile his wife in every manner imaginable, his only comfort the flask in his back pocket. He never confronted Suzanne, hoping it was a singular transgression. His continual silence was one of the complaints she listed in her letters, the envelopes containing them bearing no return address. She wrote that the war had done something to him.

She wrote he was not the same since he came back from fighting for the Confederacy.

Not the same after a war?

Hayes chuckled as he sat down behind his desk rifled with month-old reports and citations.

No man ever is, darling.

She took their baby with her. She had written in her last letter that his silences, the way he would drink from his flask and stare out the kitchen window for hours at a time, gave her indication that the child might be raised wrong if measures were not taken.

Hayes had not seen his son since and took every opportunity to avoid pondering the fact.

Herbert Scoggins sauntered in just after eight. The deputy smelled like a man who hadn't washed under his arms or between his legs for months. In truth, the degenerate likely hadn't. If it weren't for the fact that Scoggins' strange demeanor and off-putting scent and mannerisms were more of a deterrent toward law breaking than the bars of any cell, Hayes would've long ago refused to work with the man.

Scoggins removed his hat as he sat across from Hayes, a mane of curly gray hair unrolling from underneath. Scoggins with his stained suit coat eaten up by patches of various colors and designs and the permanent wince that was his face, appeared older than Hayes but in fact was three years the marshal's junior.

"Ever heard of a bath?" Hayes asked Scoggins.

Scoggins reached down his corduroy trousers and scratched. He brought the two fingers to his nose and had himself a sniff. "Ever heard of thinking ahead?"

"How does smelling like a transient rapist have anything to do with 'thinking ahead'?" Hayes, once again, found himself astounded by the words coming out of the mouth of a man he trusted with a loaded firearm and a badge.

"You ever notice how it's easier to get pussy when you're already in some?"

"I haven't even had my morning coffee yet, Herbert, and you're already throwing pussy at me."

"Someone needs to throw some at you." Scoggins coughed as he spoke.

"What was that?"

"I was telling you about my strategy."

"The 'thinking ahead.'"

"Correct. Most men get themselves some and they're happy in the moment, not thinkin' 'bout the big picture. Them's the fellas that immediately wash up. Then the other females have no idea that the fella is worth a goddamn in bed since he washed the proof off. Had he not, they'd smell it on him and know that one of their kind had recently been there, inspiring interest on the part of the as-of-yet unhumped female. That's why, after I humped on Mrs. Eliza Schultze last night—"

"Eliza Schultze?"

"She ain't married."

"She's nearing sixty."

"She don't look sixty," Scoggins said. "Must be all that hard labor she does. Changing all them sheets. Cooking, hauling them trays and linens up and down them steps day and night, not to mention the guest's luggage. She's tighter than a roll of pennies, I'll tell you that much. She also beats them brokedown whores Barmore peddles at The Brass Ass."

"The ones you and Wade frequent?" Hayes pushed the subject further away from Eliza Schultze. No good ever came from encouraging gossip that involved the town elders or members of the city council. That kind of thing cost men like Hayes—menial, replaceable public servants— their jobs.

There was also the history between Hayes and Eliza to consider. Eliza's husband had left her the boarding house on Central, the next street over, after he died in the war. For the three years following his wife and son's departure to Arkansas, Hayes and the widow had had an affair of their own. Hayes had never told anyone about his drunken, after-midnight trips to Eliza's quarters. He held a public office and had a reputation to uphold. He knew she welcomed other men into her bedroom when he wasn't around and had held no illusions about their arrangement. She had grown to love her freedom and the drummer debacle had left him without the energy or the desire to try and tame her. He ended the affair one night, drunk as usual, when she had begged him to marry her. He told her he was no longer the marrying kind, threw his clothes on and walked out on her as she lay on the damp and disheveled satin sheets, weeping. He had not had a woman since her. Simply adding half a bottle to his daily intake of alcohol had been a sufficient substitute.

"Back to my new strategy," Scoggins went on. "It's like this. You know, it's kind of like how if ye already have you a job you look better to other potential employers?"

"You've only had two jobs in your life, Herbert, and they were both basically handed to you."

"I don't appreciate that, Don." Scoggins shook his head and sat up straight, his first serious gestures and words since he'd walked through the door. "Hell, there ain't no call to talk to me like that. I don't appreciate it one bit."

"I don't care. Tompkins hired you because you're his second cousin by marriage and I hired you because no one else came knocking when I put the sign up advertising for a second deputy."

"What does any of this have to do with my strategy?"

"You're late," Hayes said. "You walk in here smelling like a vagrant. And when you say 'job' like you understand the meaning of the word, it pisses me off. The jail could have been overrun by rioters and I'd have never known it because you're late. Masterson left early, and I was asleep like I should have been because I was not scheduled for duty."

"Wade shouldn't have done that."

"He shouldn't have to stay late."

"Sorry, Don." Scoggins fiddled with his thumbs. He turned his head to the cell door standing open, leaning against the wall. "Ye sleep here last night?"

"Yeah. I mean I was around if something had come up but that ain't the point."

"I know. I just figure a bed's more comfortable."

"It's a big house. Too much empty space."

"Ye sure you don't want to hear about my strategy?"

Hayes rolled his eyes and tried to compose himself, inhaling as slowly as he could through his nose and accepting that, whether he liked it or not, he was stuck with Scoggins, and the moronic lowlife would find a way to insert the rest of his theory in some later conversation, before the shift's end. *Might as well get it over with*, Hayes thought before saying, "Go on, Herbert. Didn't mean to slow you down. Keep talking."

"The reason I didn't wash Eliza's loin juice off of me is because if I walk around smelling like musky heaven, women'll pick up the scent from miles around. They smell that pussy on ye and realize whatever ye gots worth havin' 'cause others like them've already been there. They line up to jump on it. There's a strategy if I ever heard a one, boy."

"So you're being strategic, is that what you're telling me?"

"I'm fixing on a streak. I can feel it coming on, brother."

"You're an idiot, Scoggins. The fact that no one's shot you in the face yet baffles me."

"It's hard," Scoggins cackled.

The marshal wondered how he'd restrained himself from assaulting the halfwit.

His war service had allowed him to be elected marshal but had cost him his wife and son. It had been years of bowing and sweeping, pride-swallowing hat-tipping to the ladies who lunched at the Hill House and to the likes of Walton, the whiskey-tipping councilman. The permanently ruddy-faced politician felt it appropriate to entrust Hayes with sacred duties such as pistol-whipping the Negro house boy who had allegedly defrocked Walton's wife. The councilman also paid Hayes on a daily basis to trail his three teenage daughters on their after-supper strolls, many of which included the girls teaming up against the sons of neighboring farmers in operatic barn orgies that Hayes never reported but enjoyed watching with a level of mirth and amusement rare to his lifestyle and line of work. He simply drank from his flask and observed with glee the youthful festivities.

He supposed his lot was better than the alternative, thinking of the men who had returned with empty sleeves pinned to their shirts or those who had not come home at all.

Veterans who had worn Confederate gray were welcomed back as heroes to Kentucky. Those who had fought for the Union rarely spoke of their wartime service, especially if running for office. Only Virginia and Louisiana furnished more Confederate generals, and the soul of the Commonwealth still went out to the South, prostrate like Hayes himself. The ruling class of Kentucky, or what was left of it, had attempted to remain neutral while its cities were besieged.

Cowards, a younger Hayes, diseased by illusions of glory, had conceded.

Finally, Louisville, Lexington and Frankfort fell to the Union. Hostile troops were now on the front lawns of the English-bred gentry and the broken Irish laborer alike, the latter men who'd been the first to pick up their guns to fight.

"Marshal," Scoggins snapped his fingers.

"What?" Hayes snapped back.

"You're drifting off again like some opium freak. What the hell's matter with ye?"

"Nothing."

Hayes stood and lifted his leather coat from the back of his swivel chair.

"Where you going?"

"You're two hours late and like I said, I'm past due my morning coffee."

Hayes nodded to the empty cells. "You think you can hold it down here all by your lonesome?"

"I can make a valiant attempt."

6

Don Hayes awoke in an eight-by-ten cell, one of two in the small jail, the farthest from the door. The chill in the hollow place was unpleasant. It came from the cold outside, seeping through the dank sepulchral stone that of which the cell's walls had been constructed. He leaned up on his elbows and then squatted, rubbing at his eyes with both hands, checking his mustache for snot and the bristles on his chin for saliva. Sharp pain traveled the axis of his skull when he attempted to stretch his neck.

He felt like he had been hit upside the head by one of the drunken ironworkers he often had to arrest. But the only blows he had withstood recently were courtesy of John Barleycorn and Hayes was always the instigator and loser in such quarrels.

He usually ached in the mornings, hung over or not, years of hard living finally taking their toll on him. This particular sunrise was worse than most. Every year when the weather started to turn his drinking grew worse. Maybe it was because every great loss he'd suffered occurred when the leaves were falling.

Hayes watched his father fall drunk from the roof of his

childhood home where the old man had been repairing a leak. He landed on his head, stood, said "Goddammit," and dropped dead into a pile of raked leaves. Hayes had killed his first Yankee soldier, crawling on autumn leaves to slit the throat of the sleeping private.

And the loss that had exiled him from the cold bed in his empty house to the prison cell where he slept most nights had occurred in the month of October under skeletal branches.

It was not his favorite time of year.

As his eyes adjusted to the sunlight coming through the steel bars, he wished there was a woman in his life who loved him just enough to have coffee brewing, ready for him in the morning.

Surely he was still worth that much.

He slowly tucked the brown hair he'd allowed to grow too long behind his ears. Like a child who'd burnt himself on a steam pot, he was wary of moving his head any more than he had to. He stood and plodded through the open cell door, relieved at the silence of the empty jail. He glanced at the clock above the gun rack on the far wall across from the cells.

That bastard Scoggins was late again and Masterson had left early.

He certainly hoped they weren't at church, at least not the one under the canvas of that crazy son of a bitch Thurman. The last thing he needed was to have his only two deputies in the pocket of a lunatic.

Hayes himself had fallen behind in attendance at Holy Innocents, the Catholic church on Lexington Avenue his wife had dragged him to every Sunday.

Perhaps bachelorhood did have its perks.

He would have to remember, if he ever ran into him, to thank the drummer that laid her on a haystack then swept her off to Arkansas. She sent a handful of letters detailing the matrimonial crimes he had been guilty of, blaming him for her infidelity.

Hayes had borne witness to one of the many haystack romps, months before her departure. He'd passed out drunk in his stable and woken to the sounds, never alerting them to his presence as he watched the drummer defile his wife in every manner imaginable, his only comfort the flask in his back pocket. He never confronted Suzanne, hoping it was a singular transgression. His continual silence was one of the complaints she listed in her letters, the envelopes containing them bearing no return address. She wrote that the war had done something to him.

She wrote he was not the same since he came back from fighting for the Confederacy.

Not the same after a war?

Hayes chuckled as he sat down behind his desk rifled with month-old reports and citations.

No man ever is, darling.

She took their baby with her. She had written in her last letter that his silences, the way he would drink from his flask and stare out the kitchen window for hours at a time, gave her indication that the child might be raised wrong if measures were not taken.

Hayes had not seen his son since and took every opportunity to avoid pondering the fact.

Herbert Scoggins sauntered in just after eight. The deputy smelled like a man who hadn't washed under his arms or between his legs for months. In truth, the degenerate likely hadn't. If it weren't for the fact that Scoggins' strange demeanor and off-putting scent and mannerisms were more of a deterrent toward law breaking than the bars of any cell, Hayes would've long ago refused to work with the man.

Scoggins removed his hat as he sat across from Hayes, a mane of curly gray hair unrolling from underneath. Scoggins with his stained suit coat eaten up by patches of various colors and designs and the permanent wince that was his face, appeared older than Hayes but in fact was three years the marshal's junior.

"Ever heard of a bath?" Hayes asked Scoggins.

Scoggins reached down his corduroy trousers and scratched. He brought the two fingers to his nose and had himself a sniff. "Ever heard of thinking ahead?"

"How does smelling like a transient rapist have anything to do with 'thinking ahead'?" Hayes, once again, found himself astounded by the words coming out of the mouth of a man he trusted with a loaded firearm and a badge.

"You ever notice how it's easier to get pussy when you're already in some?"

"I haven't even had my morning coffee yet, Herbert, and you're already throwing pussy at me."

"Someone needs to throw some at you." Scoggins coughed as he spoke.

"What was that?"

"I was telling you about my strategy."

"The 'thinking ahead.'"

"Correct. Most men get themselves some and they're happy in the moment, not thinkin' 'bout the big picture. Them's the fellas that immediately wash up. Then the other females have no idea that the fella is worth a goddamn in bed since he washed the proof off. Had he not, they'd smell it on him and know that one of their kind had recently been there, inspiring interest on the part of the as-of-yet unhumped female. That's why, after I humped on Mrs. Eliza Schultze last night—"

"Eliza Schultze?"

"She ain't married."

"She's nearing sixty."

"She don't look sixty," Scoggins said. "Must be all that hard labor she does. Changing all them sheets. Cooking, hauling them trays and linens up and down them steps day and night, not to mention the guest's luggage. She's tighter than a roll of pennies, I'll tell you that much. She also beats them brokedown whores Barmore peddles at The Brass Ass."

"The ones you and Wade frequent?" Hayes pushed the subject further away from Eliza Schultze. No good ever came from encouraging gossip that involved the town elders or members of the city council. That kind of thing cost men like Hayes—menial, replaceable public servants— their jobs.

There was also the history between Hayes and Eliza to consider. Eliza's husband had left her the boarding house on Central, the next street over, after he died in the war. For the three years following his wife and son's departure to Arkansas, Hayes and the widow had had an affair of their own. Hayes had never told anyone about his drunken, after-midnight trips to Eliza's quarters. He held a public office and had a reputation to uphold. He knew she welcomed other men into her bedroom when he wasn't around and had held no illusions about their arrangement. She had grown to love her freedom and the drummer debacle had left him without the energy or the desire to try and tame her. He ended the affair one night, drunk as usual, when she had begged him to marry her. He told her he was no longer the marrying kind, threw his clothes on and walked out on her as she lay on the damp and disheveled satin sheets, weeping. He had not had a woman since her. Simply adding half a bottle to his daily intake of alcohol had been a sufficient substitute.

"Back to my new strategy," Scoggins went on. "It's like this. You know, it's kind of like how if ye already have you a job you look better to other potential employers?"

"You've only had two jobs in your life, Herbert, and they were both basically handed to you."

"I don't appreciate that, Don." Scoggins shook his head and sat up straight, his first serious gestures and words since he'd walked through the door. "Hell, there ain't no call to talk to me like that. I don't appreciate it one bit."

"I don't care. Tompkins hired you because you're his second cousin by marriage and I hired you because no one else came knocking when I put the sign up advertising for a second deputy."

"What does any of this have to do with my strategy?"

"You're late," Hayes said. "You walk in here smelling like a vagrant. And when you say 'job' like you understand the meaning of the word, it pisses me off. The jail could have been overrun by rioters and I'd have never known it because you're late. Masterson left early, and I was asleep like I should have been because I was not scheduled for duty."

"Wade shouldn't have done that."

"He shouldn't have to stay late."

"Sorry, Don." Scoggins fiddled with his thumbs. He turned his head to the cell door standing open, leaning against the wall. "Ye sleep here last night?"

"Yeah. I mean I was around if something had come up but that ain't the point."

"I know. I just figure a bed's more comfortable."

"It's a big house. Too much empty space."

"Ye sure you don't want to hear about my strategy?"

Hayes rolled his eyes and tried to compose himself, inhaling as slowly as he could through his nose and accepting that, whether he liked it or not, he was stuck with Scoggins, and the moronic lowlife would find a way to insert the rest of his theory in some later conversation, before the shift's end. *Might as well get it over with*, Hayes thought before saying, "Go on, Herbert. Didn't mean to slow you down. Keep talking."

"The reason I didn't wash Eliza's loin juice off of me is because if I walk around smelling like musky heaven, women'll pick up the scent from miles around. They smell that pussy on ye and realize whatever ye gots worth havin' 'cause others like them've already been there. They line up to jump on it. There's a strategy if I ever heard a one, boy."

"So you're being strategic, is that what you're telling me?"

"I'm fixing on a streak. I can feel it coming on, brother."

"You're an idiot, Scoggins. The fact that no one's shot you in the face yet baffles me."

"It's hard," Scoggins cackled.

The marshal wondered how he'd restrained himself from assaulting the halfwit.

His war service had allowed him to be elected marshal but had cost him his wife and son. It had been years of bowing and sweeping, pride-swallowing hat-tipping to the ladies who lunched at the Hill House and to the likes of Walton, the whiskey-tipping councilman. The permanently ruddy-faced politician felt it appropriate to entrust Hayes with sacred duties such as pistol-whipping the Negro house boy who had allegedly defrocked Walton's wife. The councilman also paid Hayes on a daily basis to trail his three teenage daughters on their after-supper strolls, many of which included the girls teaming up against the sons of neighboring farmers in operatic barn orgies that Hayes never reported but enjoyed watching with a level of mirth and amusement rare to his lifestyle and line of work. He simply drank from his flask and observed with glee the youthful festivities.

He supposed his lot was better than the alternative, thinking of the men who had returned with empty sleeves pinned to their shirts or those who had not come home at all.

Veterans who had worn Confederate gray were welcomed back as heroes to Kentucky. Those who had fought for the Union rarely spoke of their wartime service, especially if running for office. Only Virginia and Louisiana furnished more Confederate generals, and the soul of the Commonwealth still went out to the South, prostrate like Hayes himself. The ruling class of Kentucky, or what was left of it, had attempted to remain neutral while its cities were besieged.

Cowards, a younger Hayes, diseased by illusions of glory, had conceded.

Finally, Louisville, Lexington and Frankfort fell to the Union. Hostile troops were now on the front lawns of the English-bred gentry and the broken Irish laborer alike, the latter men who'd been the first to pick up their guns to fight.

"Marshal," Scoggins snapped his fingers.

"What?" Hayes snapped back.

"You're drifting off again like some opium freak. What the hell's matter with ye?"

"Nothing."

Hayes stood and lifted his leather coat from the back of his swivel chair.

"Where you going?"

"You're two hours late and like I said, I'm past due my morning coffee."

Hayes nodded to the empty cells. "You think you can hold it down here all by your lonesome?"

"I can make a valiant attempt."

7

The mute washed off what remained of Jessup in a still-water pool just before the last stretch of mountain. All she had of him now was the souvenir she'd affixed to her mare the night before. It was all that men like him deserved to leave behind. The Apaches were more liberal with their application of the treatment. There were a lot of things she had learned from them that she had made her own. It was a thread that ran through her life like the blood that mixed with the water as she soaked her shirt from the creek bed where she stood shivering.

It wasn't a bath but it would do.

They were still far from civilization. They had slept little and eaten less. She lifted the shirt from the water, ringing it out, and ran it once more along her breasts, neck, and stomach. She discarded the useless garment into the water and buttoned her coat around her bare midriff before shambling up the bank.

They had stolen a wool coat and a snap-button shirt for her on a clothesline in the backyard of a farmer's house on the eastern fringes of Mercy. Between the rows of drying sheets and comforters she quickly discarded her bloody coat and changed while Tompal and Cody kept watch.

She held her arms upturned and outstretched before her, wearing a verecund smile as she presented her new wardrobe for the two men to critique.

"Not bad," Tompal said.

"Ye getting' respectable on us, girl," Cody said.

She blushed and batted her eyes.

Schultze's Boarding House was a gray two-story affair with a gabled roof, identical to half of the other buildings on Central Avenue. The foyer's oak floors and panels remained free of dust or clutter. The sterile ambiance made Tompal nervous, reminded him of a prison with expensive fixtures. He had not been in such a first-class establishment in years and felt underdressed to say the least. He had wiped his feet on the doormat but still managed to track in some mud. The lady behind the counter took notice, clearing her throat and cocking her eyebrows as if the gestures would make the dirty man feel awkward enough to turn and walk out the way he'd come.

"How much for a room?" Tompal asked.

"Just one?" The lady glared at Tompal and company like they were lepers covered in lesions with missing fingers, ears, and noses.

"Just one," Tompal said.

Eliza Schultze's corset constricted her cleavage into a display package. Her gown was red velvet. She'd become known for wearing red as it matched her hair. The proprietress chewed on her lower lip then nodded to the two standing on the porch, visible through the foyer window, the Negro and the girl in the black derby hat, both standing as if on guard, scanning the thoroughfare for any kind of threat. Eliza quickly ascertained that these three were undesirables and might bring with them, along with their stench and filth, a worse kind of trouble. She knew the perfect way to send them off, something socially acceptable in these parts that the white man would have to understand. Surely he'd run into complications as a result of travelling with a Negro before.

"What about the nigger?" Eliza nodded to the window and Tompal's companions beyond.

"What about him?"

"I don't normally allow them."

"You said 'normally'? That means sometimes you make exceptions."

"What is your relationship to the nigger?"

"We ain't related. Like you already pointed out, he's a nigger."

"I mean, why are you traveling together?"

"Since I'm the one who is lowering my standards by offering this third-rate establishment my business, why don't you allow me a question? On what rare occasions do you allow Negroes to sleep under this roof?"

"When people once had slaves accompany them we'd allowed Negroes to sleep in the cellar. Nowadays, I'll occasionally get a guest who travels with a servant and we'll extend to them the same courtesy."

"That's mighty hospitable of you. Well, that nigger outside is my servant so he can stay. But I won't have him in the cellar."

"He must stay in the cellar."

"That just won't do. I need him by my side at all times. I can't be calling for you to run down and fetch him every time I need him to decipher Morse code."

"Morse code?"

"Yes. I don't know Morse code. What if an urgent telegram comes and it needs deciphering? Waiting for him to decipher it is suspenseful enough without having to add the time it takes him to travel two stories."

"That nigger takes Morse code?"

"Honey, that nigger can tap dance Morse code faster than most white people can write it down. It's as if he has a mind of his own sometimes. I'm sad to say it but it's almost like I'm useless without him. What if I begin to get homesick and need a soothing hymn sung to me? By the time he makes it to my room I could be a weeping train wreck. What if an idea comes and by the time he arrives at my door to write it down for me I've forgotten it. Are you willing to shoulder that kind of responsibility?"

"What kind of business are you in, Mr..."

Tompal stared at her cleavage.

"Do the Appalachians there remain so youthful lookin' naturally or is there a secret?"

Her jaw fell agape and she covered her breasts with both hands.

"Did it make growin' up hard? You expandin' while all them other little girls only sprouted about a handful of titty?"

Tompal held up his palm and squeezed an invisible breast.

"Did that offend you..." Tompal glanced at the sign above her window. "Mrs. Schultze? You Schultze?"

She nodded yes.

"This your place?"

"It was my husband's."

"Was?"

"He passed on, if you must know."

"Died in the war?"

"Sir, I don't exactly feel the need to share—"

"Mrs. Schultze."

"What?"

"You didn't answer my question."

"Which question?"

"Did I offend you?"

"Yes, you did. You spoke to me in a way I have never—"

"Because I crossed a line. A boundary. Without being invited to do so."

"I would say so."

"It wasn't none of my business how you got your titties to do like that."

"I don't know why you feel the need to speak to me in this manner. All I—"

"So you now know where I'm coming from when I ask you to kindly keep your nose out of my affairs."

She opened her mouth a few times to speak, placing her hands on her hips and stepping back from the counter, cocking her head over her left shoulder. She was confounded for she could not begin to form a response to the stranger standing in her foyer.

It was the first time she could remember that she had failed to learn at least a few pieces of gossip. It was also the first time a guest knew more about her than she did him.

The three shared the double bed. The mute lay between the two men, Cody taking the first watch, leaning against the bedpost with his rifle on his lap.

Sharing the room was not debated. They had learned early not to make easy the work of violent pursuers, dividing for the conquerors before they even invaded. With the three sharing not just quarters but a bed, taking turns sleeping, no adversary could so much as step into the hall outside unnoticed. With the watchman right beside those sleeping, the vulnerable parties could be awakened at a moment's notice.

They only planned to be in town a day, to sleep on a mattress instead of wet grass or dirt, to bathe and then be on their way deeper into the Commonwealth.

8

The couple sitting before Scoggins in the marshal's office had interrupted the deputy's lunch, a bit of rum in his coffee and a few hand-rolled cigarettes. They also caused Scoggins' stomach to turn, not so much their stoic posture, but their collective, lifeless gaze.

The man was in his fifties at least, frail and sallow, his thick, white hair coalescing in a ponytail that rested on his right shoulder. His wife, seated beside him, was at least a quarter century younger and by far the more masculine of the two. Broad-shouldered, she'd kept her raven hair cropped close, her short, dark tufts disheveled from where she had removed her hat. She dressed in denim trousers and a Navy pea coat. It was as if they had switched roles, her as the husband and him the wife, bowing and scraping behind her. She even did the talking while she held the unfurled wanted poster in place on Scoggins' desk for him to view.

"Where did you find this?" Scoggins asked.

"It was posted in the sheriff's office. Had been for a week," the wife said.

"That says Virginia. You just said you come from West

Virginia." Scoggins flicked a curled edge of the yellow paper.

"The last town they shot up in Virginia had the wherewithal to send this poster our way since that was the direction they was last seen ridin'. It's kind of like what we're doin' here, givin' you warnin' that these three might be comin' through here and they ain't the type you want droppin' in on you unexpected."

"So now they're guilty of crimes in two states."

"Maybe three if you don't get up off your ass and start doing what this town pays you for."

"Ma'am, there's no reason to jump straight from prim and proper to ornery just because I make a few humble inquiries. What kind of deputy would I be if I just went hunting for blood every time someone came into this jail asking me to? For all I know you made this shit up yerself."

"I beg your pardon?"

"Now you're begging? Well, that's more like it, hon."

"Where's the sheriff?"

"We ain't got a sheriff."

"You said you were a deputy. There's always something above the deputy."

"We got a marshal."

"Very well. I want to speak to the marshal then"

"He won't be back for a while. You may want to stop by later on in the day."

"Where is he?"

"As you can see, ma'am, he's out."

"Doing what?"

"Marshalling."

"I want to speak to him."

"He gets that a lot. Hell of a conversationalist, Marshal

Hayes."

"These three brigands kilt my husbands' brother. He was a decorated Confederate veteran, a sheriff. They rode west. The only state west in any damn direction is Kentucky. This is the first town we come to."

"May I be allowed one more question?"

"Could the grace of providence itself stop you?"

"How did these three pass through your town without hindrance, if posters such as this were all over the Virginias?"

Scoggins placed his elbows on the table, resting one arm over the other and squinted, his face hovering just above the poster, making a big show of examining the three faces crudely drawn side by side: an older white-haired Negro, a bushy-haired white man who looked to be in his mid- to late thirties, and a much younger female, pubescent perhaps, with markings on her face. There were three sets of lines under each eye, running from the top of her cheekbones down to her jaw.

"What is that?" Scoggins pointed to the marking, "Is that some sort of war paint? She Indian?"

"No," the wife said. "She's a white woman. Those are tattoos. They're blue."

"Blue tattoos? On her face? That's something you don't see every day."

"So is killing four people in cold blood in broad daylight."

The girl's hair was shorter than either of the men's, the whites of her eyes shadowed by her derby hat, her sex only determinable by her pouty lips and the cleavage the amateur artist had crudely included at the bottom of her profile.

The face in the middle, the portrait of the white man, was the only one with a name written under it. TOMPAL

BANKS screamed out in capital letters, under which the reader was informed that he and the other two were wanted in the state of Virginia for the crimes of murder, robbery, destruction of private property, assault, and trespassing.

"These three seem kind of hard to overlook," Scoggins added.

"Only one of them remained present among us." The man who had identified himself as Clyde Tanner spoke for the first time since introducing himself, tapping the girl's profile with his index finger.

"She's a mute," Mrs. Tanner said. "Pat Mulhall, the man who owns the local saloon, said so. He poured her whiskey right before she butchered two of his customers."

The Tanner woman then pointed back and forth to the portraits of the Negro and the white man.

"While the mute girl was keeping an eye on a man, a blacksmith by the name of Nathan Eble at Mulhall's, these two robbed his house then rode in and picked up their accomplice but not before murdering the two in the bar, then Eble and the sheriff in the broad daylight, right in front of the whole damned town. I was there myself. I witnessed them kill the sheriff and Eble with my own two eyes. How many times am I gonna have to tell the story before you decide to go and look for them?"

"What did they steal from Eble's house?"

"What?" Mrs. Tanner said.

"What did they steal? Did they steal antiques? Gold? What? You said he was a blacksmith. If I was going to steal it'd be from a wealthy cattle farmer or a bank for that matter."

"I didn't get the details on what was stolen from Eble. But they killed him. And they killed three other people.

Ain't that reason enough to be alarmed?"

"Why am I not speaking to two—"

"Two who? Two lawmen? The sheriff is dead, Deputy. These three kilt him. His deputy is a halfwit drunk who'd rather sleep off a hangover than do his job and notify the next civilized area that hell is about to reign down upon them. For all we know he's allowing our community to be ravaged by niggers and charlatans as we speak. Come to think of it, he reminds me a lot of you, Deputy Scoggins. Maybe you two could meet up for a cow buggering if you ever find yerself in our corner of the world."

"Mrs. Tanner!"

"We have taken it upon ourselves as good Samaritans to come here and inform you of the kind of wretched spawn of the nether regions that is coming your way and you have the temerity to sit there all lazy-eyed and slack-jawed, grinning like a goddamn Yankee who just heard tell of Lee's surrender."

"Sir." Scoggins looked at Mr. Tanner, refusing to address the woman. "I've listened to about enough of this. If you don't get your wife under control, I'm going to do so myself."

She rolled up the wanted poster and stormed out without waiting for her husband, who sat for another moment smiling sheepishly at the giggling deputy.

"We'll look into it," Scoggins said between snorts of laughter.

It was now apparent that the revitalizing effect Clyde Tanner first believed this trip West could have on his marriage would be, at best, negligible. His wife had not said two words to him since they crossed the state line.

Geraldine had, two weeks ago, in his presence, sat before her mirror in their bedroom, gripped several locks of her long raven black hair and, revealing a dagger in her other hand, freed herself of her last vestiges of femininity, already having made a show of strutting around town in a Stetson hat and denim trousers.

He should have known when he tried to straddle her face on their wedding night and she bit the head of his pecker so hard that the teeth marks were still visible, that there was something different about the woman. He knew something to be amiss for sure when he came home from a long day at the funeral home to find her and the octoroon maid in the throes of an alien embrace, naked, each one's head to the other's loins, sucking and gyrating like two cannibalistic serpents.

He'd watched without their detection, unzipping his pants and abusing himself, aroused by the unholy ceremony conducted in his living room.

Today, as he trailed behind her through the mud alleys of Mercy, he wondered why she had grown so righteously indignant at the injustice that had befallen the Tanner family. It was not her brother. She, in fact, despised the late Sheriff Tanner, a gluttonous philistine as she had called him to his face at many a family function.

It could have been some strange form of repentance. She'd been raised Catholic by a father who beat her bloody with his walking cane every time she made eye contact with a male houseguest, accusing her of batting eyes. She might have thought that bringing these three to justice, stopping whatever carnage and chaos they might continue to orchestrate was her tithing, her insurance against damnation. Perhaps she believed that if she prevented the three outlaws from repeating the massacre in front of Mulhall's, she could go on licking and munching until the end of the world without fear of God's bloody walking cane.

Whatever the particulars, Clyde was certain that when his wife watched from the crowd, while the three killed Eble and his brother, something was dislodged deep inside her.

9

Jack Peterson sat at a corner table in Mulhall's saloon where Cal and Jessup Naughton had been massacred two days before. Peterson's boss, Sheriff Tanner, and the blacksmith, Nathan Eble, had fallen to the same fate just outside the saloon. Luckily for him, Peterson had been off duty and inebriated when the unfortunate incident had occurred.

Townspeople and shop owners returned to life as usual, getting along with their daily errands, running back and forth between their churches, banks, and bars. At a young age, Peterson had discerned that every town his gambling man of a father brought him through turned out to be the same. One day, leaving Carthage, Illinois, young Peterson asked his senior, "Daddy, how come everywhere we go all we see is churches, banks, and bars?" His father got a good laugh out of his green little mini-gambler's inquiry before answering, "Boy, you gonna spend the rest of your life figuring that out."

Miners came in to spend on drink and lust what they had just earned in the mountains that supported the town. Life went on just as it always had without the four that had been lost.

Peterson's hands shook as he downed the last of his three o'clock bourbon, his first drink of the day.

Since Tanner had been killed Peterson had become acting sheriff and felt that imbibing before five was unbecoming of man in his new and esteemed position.

Geraldine Tanner, the dyke that had somehow managed to snag the now-dead sheriff's brother in a state of matrimony, had stormed into the jail hours after the shootings, insisting that he gather a posse and mount up to ride after the three killers. While her castrated husband, Clyde Tanner, stood silently by, Peterson politely rejected her suggestion, feeling that it was not part of his job to pressure citizens to take arms and venture into other states pursuing violent offenders and that the town had suffered enough loss.

When she saw their wanted poster pinned to the jail wall she went to pieces, shouting that if he wouldn't bring the three killers to justice, she would find someone who would.

She stormed out of the jail leaving her slack-shouldered husband to study the floor beams awkwardly before tipping his hat goodbye to Peterson and walking out after her.

Good riddance, Peterson thought, pouring another taste from the complimentary bottle that sat before him, one of the many perks a sheriff should rightly enjoy with the stresses he shouldered in a day's work. He savored the calm warmth of the liquor, the moment quickly interrupted by the creak of the saloon doors.

Two men stood in the shadows of the doorway, their features darkened by the dim saloon, sunset barely finding welcome through the doors and small windows. They wore black overcoats and Stetsons, both skinny and pale like men who conducted most of their business indoors.

They scanned the room like owls, their eyes moving with their skulls as if one pulled the other. Upon spotting Peterson alone in the corner, their tandem pivoting gaze stopped in unison. The one with the mustache grinned, eyeing the tin star.

They approached the new sheriff's table, standing on either side of him.

"Peterson," the one with the black mustache curling over his upper lip said. He spoke with a Midwestern accent.

"Who's askin'?" Peterson filled his glass for the third time.

"I wasn't askin'," the same one said. "The old sheriff was shot down like a dog in the street outside this time two days ago. We were told his deputy, one Jack Peterson, is the acting sheriff now and in fact the only law in a thirty-mile radius. You're wearing a star. You're Peterson."

The mustached man pulled out the chair before him and sat down, nodding at his associate.

The clean-shaven man sat and eyed Peterson. He appeared in a perpetual state of dissatisfaction.

Peterson noticed the scar that ran down the left side of the shaven man's face, from the far corner of his yellowy eye to his chin.

"Now do me a favor, Sheriff Peterson," he continued. "Make that be the last time in this conversation you force me to state the obvious."

"Excuse me?"

"Is that really necessary? I would much rather move right along to the matter at hand. As I was saying before you so rudely interrupted me, my name is Mr. McMahon. This is Mr. Sleadd, my lieutenant. This is not our first visit to this modern Philistia but we hope it will be our last. This part of the country makes me ill. It's a backwater full of illiterates and inbreeds. We made this last trip from Cleveland with the purpose of purchasing an antique collection from the late Nathan Eble. We had already made an advance payment only to discover him dead and the goods for which we'd already put cash down missing from his home, where we were to meet him and exchange the rest of the money."

Peterson opened his mouth to speak.

"I'm not finished." McMahon held up an index finger, halting Peterson's interruption. "As you already know the house was broken into. What you do not know is what was taken. And how could you? Eble, I'm sure, did not leave a checklist of belongings at the sheriff station before passing. You had no frame of reference. We do. And our inspection yielded disturbing results."

"Now hold on a goddamn minute. Who do ye think you are? You can't just go snooping around people's houses. I don't care if they are dead or what you say your interest may—"

McMahon nodded to Sleadd who stood up and slapped Peterson across his face. Peterson went for his gun but Sleadd took hold of his wrist and forced his hand to the table.

"Hey." A dirty-faced, drunken miner stood from the bar and approached. Mulhall, behind the bar, shook his head as he scrubbed the inner rim of a glass.

"Stay out of it," he said to the miner.

"You leave him be." The miner took another step.

Sleadd tucked back the flap of his overcoat to reveal a black leather shoulder holster harnessing dragoons under either arm. He touched the handle of one gun and eyed the miner.

"Jesus." The miner reclaimed his seat at the bar. "What the hell's the matter with people these days?"

"I don't know," Mulhall said, without looking up. The only thing on Mulhall's mind in that moment was figuring ways to leave the South, to expedite the sale of his business and get on his way to Montana where he could assist his cousin on the successful cattle ranch he had started. He didn't want any trouble.

But trouble had a way of showing up whether a man wanted it or not. McMahon now stood, brandishing a large blade.

Peterson went for his revolver. As Sleadd forced Peterson's free hand to the table, McMahon reached down and disarmed the new sheriff, whipping him once with the barrel then tossing the gun under the table.

"I already told you who we were, Sheriff. I asked you not to make me repeat myself." McMahon brought the blade down, pinning Peterson's hand to the table.

Peterson screamed like an animal, his voice breaking, tears cascading down his face. He grabbed the blade's handle, trying to free his bleeding hand from the table but upon the slightest movement, thunderbolts of pain soared from his fingertips to his wrist. He leaned to his left and regurgitated on the sawdust floor.

"Peterson." McMahon hovered over the vomiting lawman.

Peterson continued to lean, watery eyed and fading from consciousness.

"Peterson, you useless bastard," McMahon slapped him again, an act which, with the force of gravity, knocked him out of his chair, cutting his hand in half lengthwise as it pulled free of the blade, still embedded deep in the table.

Peterson keeled over into the fetal position, holding his ruined hand against his stomach, bloodying his shirt and pants, stifled whimpers emanating from his trembling mouth.

"Looks like a goddamn flipper." McMahon laughed, pointing to Peterson's split-down-the-middle hand, exposing bone and veins that gushed dark blood all over the town's new sheriff, who turned white where he lay.

"Was that a sufficient introduction?" McMahon squatted over Peterson. "Now, if you will please tell us everything you know about the three who killed Nathan Eble."

10

"You let them walk out of here?" Hayes said, black coffee steaming from the tin cup in his hand.

"You should've seen 'em, Marshal." Scoggins still refused to take the situation seriously. "Craziest lookin' people I ever saw in my life save the reverend. It don't add up. None of it. Three degenerates shoot up a town, come riding into our state and we get notified by a couple of circus folk? She looked like the man and he looked the woman. What stock could she possibly have in such a mess as she described. It was the husband's brother that was supposed to be one of the victims. They're playing some sort of prank on us. Probably go from town to town besieging decent folks with their horseshit. I bet it's the only thing keeping their prison cell of a marriage from going to hell. He's probably watching her abuse herself as we speak."

"Scoggins, when I was at the boarding house this morning getting my first cup—"

"You've been gone a while, Marshal. Get into anything?"

"I had to talk to Newmyer again. Now listen to me, Scoggins."

He had seen Lacey, the young bride of Mercy's only

undertaker, a demonic drunk by the name of Christopher Newmyer. She'd been slogging down Central Avenue with her head lowered, a bruise the size of Missouri around her left eye.

"That shitheel. You straighten him out?" Scoggins interrupted again.

"I talked to him. Scoggins—"

"That took you all morning."

"Some other things came up. Listen to me now. I was at the boarding house this morning getting my coffee and Mrs. Schultze—"

"That shot of life. The images that come to mind now at the mere mention of dear Eliza. I could write a book, Marshal."

"Shut up, Scoggins. Shut your goddamn mouth right now before I shoot your teeth out the back of your head."

"Jesus."

"While she was readying my morning coffee, Eliza Schultze was going on about the new guests that had just arrived."

"Women? Maybe I should head over and let them get a whiff of my love scent."

"Two men. One woman. A girl. A girl with blue tattoos under both eyes. One of the men was a Negro with white hair. The other was a white man. He had bad manners and bushy black hair, sprinkles of white in it."

Scoggins stood and rushed to the gun rack. Hayes took a long pull off his coffee, set the tin cup on his desk, and stepped beside Scoggins before the rifles and shotguns as the deputy loaded a Winchester.

Hayes drew his revolver, thumbed the hammer down halfway, spinning the cylinder to make sure every chamber held a round.

"Scoggins, you stupid son of a bitch."

Tompal woke to Cody's guttural snoring, the old black man's lips specked with drying saliva that his tongue re-moistened every few minutes.

The mute, last on watch, handed him the rifle and nodded to the door.

"You want a proper bath now, I guess." Tompal's boot-heels touched the dustless floor.

The mute nodded as she sat up next to Tompal. She held her revolver limply in her lap.

"Okay. I'll run downstairs for you and have it fetched. We'll all take turns washin'. Then we'll have us some sup-per while Mrs. Schultze puts some clean linens on this bed we just muddied up."

The mute and Tompal both examined the bed, dirtied by the dry leaves and mountain dirt they'd brought with them.

"Serves her right, the nosy old bitch." Tompal stood and retrieved his suit coat from the rack beside the bed.

The mute stood naked in the middle of the room when Tompal returned to tell her the bath was on its way, that it would be brought to the communal washroom down the hall for her.

She squatted, untying her canvas tote bag and retrieving the satin robe Tompal and Cody had brought her from their conquest of the blacksmith's house.

Cody had also taken the blacksmith's Union blues, simply to add insult to injury. Tompal had asked why Cody was so set against the North, them being the ones that set his people free.

"I don't like being lied to." he'd said.

"Lied to? Lincoln done freed the slaves, Cody. I don't see no Negroes wearing shackles no more."

"They find ways."

"They are without question gaping assholes of the highest magnitude. I just figured you might have leaned toward the North, being that they seemed to have had some of your interests at heart."

"They all the same. Now they just put us in prison on horseshit charges and get their goddamn free labor that way. Are we citizens? Shit no. We either wind up jailed or strung up to prove a point. That war wasn't about no slaves or right or wrong. It was about rich white assholes getting richer. And who do you think died so that could happen?"

"I got a feeling it wasn't a rich, white asshole."

"No. It was a poor, stupid hillbilly or a black-ass nigger like me who done believed some asshole's bullshit. And the North used that horseshit to sell more of it, sayin' 'Look, we care about the Negroes so much we even lettin' 'em die for us so we can make sure the South don't make no money without us getting our taste.' That don't sound like change to me. And who you think sets that interest so high that almost every family we seen in every town from here to Selma is livin' in shacks, their kids dirty and shoeless now that the war's over and they know they got the penniless South over the barrel?"

"I don't know, Cody. You always understood these things better than me."

"The Yankees,. All them banks is based up North. Clean the shit out yer ears. It's a rigged deck. We're just food for the worms as far as they's concerned."

"So why you want a Northern uniform?"

"I'm goin' put it to good use."

"Good use?"

"By depriving a rich, white asshole of it."

Now, a sleeping Cody was stripped down to his long johns. He continued snoring while Tompal entered the room again.

"Bath's on its way," Tompal said to the mute. He then glanced back at Cody. "Damn, he's loud. It's a wonder we slept at all. We should order up some rope and tie his jaw shut."

The mute laughed at Tompal's joke as she wrapped herself in satin. She tucked a towel beneath one arm, her soiled jeans and new shirt folded under the other and opened the door to the hallway.

11

As she dried, the bathwater had turned blackish brown with islands of dirt and lint clinging to her well-turned ankles. She left the used towel in the hamper and hitched her britches around her waist. She draped her new flannel shirt over her shoulders, leaving it unbuttoned as she opened the door, the robe tucked under her arm.

She stepped into the hallway, appraising her cracked, blistered feet, her yellow toenails ate up by some fungus she'd caught out West. She looked up to see a man and woman blocking the way to her door. The woman had short hair, wore men's denim and flannel like the mute but clearly by choice, for her skin remained flawless, her scent perfumed, far from that of a woman who had lived an entire life of hard times or been put upon by the vagaries of fate. Her companion, slack-shouldered and sallow, appeared well-to-do, dressed up in a brand-new tweed suit with long, shiny hair kept in a ponytail.

The mute smiled and moved forward hoping they would allow her by. The woman took a step back to complement the mute's movement, tugging the man's coat.

"It's her, Clyde." The mute saw the woman's eyes fill

with an, excited, raging lust, the same expression the mute had seen on the two men who'd tried to have their way with her in that West Virginia mining town.

Clyde stood frozen. If there was a cue to be taken, he had surely missed it. The mute stopped not a foot before Clyde, eyeballing him.

The woman tugged harder on his sleeve.

"Goddammit, Clyde! You just gonna stand there? She killed your brother."

Clyde unbuttoned his coat to reveal the butt of a .44 revolver jutting out of his waistband.

"We don't know if it's her." He glanced at the woman.

"Jesus Christ." Geraldine Tanner grabbed the pistol grip and began to pull, but Clyde's belt was tight. The cylinder caught. The mute dropped her robe and her dirty linens and kicked the woman's hand that held the gun, her heel hitting Clyde's crotch.

Clyde groaned and the woman let out a whimper but did not release her grip. She kept struggling, knocking the .44's hammer down in the process.

The mute kicked again.

Clyde's left thigh exploded with a crack into a rosebud of muscle and artery, his pants catching fire. He collapsed against the banister, slapping at his pant leg with both hands to put the fire out.

While Clyde examined what she had done to him, the woman stared aghast at her male companion, the smoking gun in her hands. She glanced up expecting to see the girl with scars under her eyes, instead finding her vision eclipsed by an approaching fist.

* * *

Tompal stepped into the hallway, the rifle extended.

"There just ain't no end to it?" Tompal glanced at the two bodies in the hallway, the mute standing on the other side of them.

The mute looked back down at the woman she had just slugged and saw the revolver rising, the cold-blue eyes, one reddening now, staring up at her from behind the short curtain of raven hair.

The mute turned and sprinted back to the washroom. She dove onto the checkerboard floor right as the gaslight attached to the hallway ceiling shattered. Knocking over the tin bathtub, she was submerged by a flood of dirty water. She flipped onto her back and kicked the door closed as the second shot sounded and splintered the lower door-frame. The round embedded itself in the upturned tub, missing her by inches as she curled into the corner, her hands over her ears.

Tompal had his back to the women, retreating to the bedroom to tell Cody that they would be checking out early. Two more shots echoed through the hallway just as he made it to the bed.

Cody dropped to the floor as Tompal backed up against the dresser in the room's corner. He slid down, pulling his knees to his chest.

Tompal edged toward the door and peeked into the hall.

A brutish woman in her mid-twenties balanced herself, her back against the wall, one hand on the banister over the dead man. A .44 revolver dangled loosely in the other. She spotted Tompal and lifted the .44. He retreated into the room as the shot knocked loose the brass doorknob from its hole.

"She alive?" Cody squatted next to Tompal.

"Last I checked. And she can shoot, too"

"How many?" Cody whispered.

"There were two I saw. But they were both on the ground like maybe she had gotten the drop on them."

"Then who's shootin'?

"Maybe there was more where them two came from. Maybe someone came out from one of them other rooms down the hall."

"Shit, we cornered."

"Don't panic."

Another round pierced through the wall next to the dresser, a spiderweb forming across the northern window that provided a view of Central.

Cody cupped his ears and cursed.

"I knew we shoulda kept on," Tompal muttered.

"We needed bed rest. I'm tired. Tired of sleeping on dew-wet grass and fuckin' mud like we been I don't know how long."

"Goddamnit, this is not the time for debate, Cody."

"I don't want to die here. I promised myself a long time ago I wouldn't die in the South."

"So you want to die up North? I thought you hated those assholes."

"I ain't never been to California."

"Jesus Christ. You think there aren't assholes in California."

"I don't want to die in the South, Tompal. I don't want these short-dicked sons of bitches stringing me up the same place where every shitty thing that could happen to a man befell me. Can't ye understand that?"

"Would you please shut up?"

"And I can't find my goddamn clothes to save my own

life. Did you hide 'em, you asshole?"

The next bullet ricocheted off the brass bedpost, burying itself in the top dresser drawer half a foot above Cody's head. He hit the deck, crawling to the mute's satchel where he'd stored the stolen Yankee uniform.

Cody opened the window that looked out onto the mud alley below and threw down the blacksmith's folded uniform.

"What are you doing?"

"Slippin' out the back way before they can drag me out the front."

"She's still in there."

"She'll either make it or she won't, Tompal. Us dyin' too ain't gon' help her none."

Tompal stood and headed toward the door.

"You crazy son of a bitch." Cody pulled on his boots and crawled out holding onto the windowsill with his fingers, dangling like a man on the end of a noose.

Tompal entered a hallway empty of life. The crumpled man leaning against the banister was dead, blood coagulating in a pool several feet wide around him.

Bloody footprints leading from the dead man to the stairs told Tompal that there was only one pursuer who had clearly fled. Tompal stepped over the dead man and around the blood, and made his way to the bathroom door. He knocked with the stock of the Colt.

The door slowly creaked open and there she stood, drenched in dirty bathwater, a sag in her shoulders, wearing that same unimpressed look; she could have just prepared a pot roast as easily as she had survived a shootout.

"Make sure you don't leave nothing behind." Tompal lowered the rifle. "Cody's gone."

12

They found the Tanner woman in the middle of Central Avenue in front of the boarding house, lying in the muddy thoroughfare, prone and catatonic.

Reverend Thurman was repeating scripture to the woman covered in blood, telling her about the kingdom of heaven and the meek inheriting the earth. He lifted her in his arms.

Customers from Tompkins General Store, many still in their Sunday best and just released from services at Holy Innocents, gathered to listen and watch alongside the whores in their pastel gowns, flooding out of The Brass Ass, chalk-white faces beneath hats covered in red roses and black cherries.

"Stand aside, Reverend," Hayes interrupted Thurman, getting down on bended knee. He pushed the reverend away as he placed his hand at the back of Tanner's head, catching her as she fell away from Thurman. He slowly lowered her, allowing her to lay on the cold mud so he could examine her for injuries.

"I am witnessing here, Marshal," Thurman yelled as he stood.

Hayes looked up at him.

"I am trying to track three wanted killers, Reverend, and to see if this woman is hurt. She may be in need of immediate medical attention, which, in my experience, the Lord don't have that great a record of providin'. So if you don't mind—"

"We are just passing through this world, Marshal. I am trying to save this woman's immortal soul while she is in a susceptible state."

"Just doesn't seem fair does it, Thurman. What with her all bloody and trauma-ridden? Ripe and ready to be filled with the Holy Spirit and all I can think about is her health."

"Might we be of some assistance, Marshal?" a voice called from behind Hayes.

Hayes rose and turned to the crowd to see the entire Mills gang standing in the forefront: Ike, Erastus, Deke Hagstaff and Roy Thompson, their Sunday best failing to civilize them in the mind of the man who had turned a blind eye to their hellraising for over ten years because they never overstepped the county line, another regret Hayes still harbored.

"If y'all would just kindly escort yer reverend to his original destination," Hayes said to Ike, the one who had spoken, "me and Scoggins would be obliged."

"The reverend'll go wherever he pleases, Marshal," Ike said. "He saved my daddy's life and his eternal soul."

"Oh, I forgot," Hayes said. "Y'all are saved now."

"I wouldn't bellyache too much, Hayes," Deke said. "It ain't like you ever arrested us. You just turned the other cheek almost like a Christian would and went after one of them ironworkers instead. I guess you was scared of getting yourself hurt. Us hurtin' Shaky Hayes? What do you think of that, Ike?"

"What did you call me?" Hayes looked at Deke. "What?"

"You called me Shaky? Where'd that come from?"

"Aw hell, Hayes," Ike said. "It's just a little name we made up for you. You know you tremble a little bit. You ain't noticed that? Like when you're nervous or when you're mad or when you gotta make a decision or when you ain't had your hourly shot of whiskey. We didn't mean nothin' by it."

Hayes now took notice that his hands were shaking at his side. What frightened him wasn't the shaking. This was not news. He had done it since the war, more so after his wife left. It was one of those things one learned to live with. He had gotten to the point where he ceased to even notice. What frightened him was that at this moment he did not know which factor Ike described was the contributing one.

"I don't know why you're so hard on Thurman," Roy said. "He's doing a great thing for this community. You ought to think about comin' down on Sundays your own self, Hayes. It ain't like God's the one took yer wife and son from you."

Hayes ran at them, his hand on his gun.

"Don." Scoggins wrapped his arms around the marshal from behind, planting his boots firmly in the mud below.

"Leave now," Scoggins screamed over the foul tirade emanating from the mouth of the incensed marshal.

Thurman took a few steps backward, shifted his boots, and scurried south down Central toward his tent while the Mills gang mounted their horses in front of Tompkins.

"We'll be seeing you, Shaky." Ike tipped his hat as they

began their trek west on Central toward the city's outskirts.

The marshal struggled free and knelt over the Tanner woman again.

"What happened here?" He felt her body for wounds, quickly surmising that the blood covering her belonged to someone else.

She turned her head and raised her index finger to the steps leading to the boarding-house porch, at two of the same faces she had pointed at less than an hour earlier as she pled for assistance to prevent such tragedy as had befallen her.

"That's them," Scoggins whispered, chambering a round into his Winchester.

Hayes stood up straight and met eyes with the girl.

The blue tattoos were covered with dirt and lint, and her black derby hat was cocked at an angle as if thrown on in a hurry. But it was definitely her.

Hayes shifted his gaze to her male escort, who had a pump rifle slung across his shoulders. He was possessed of a calm as he stared down at the armed marshal and deputy, and then at the Tanner woman. Tompal Banks acted as if none of this were abnormal.

"We were just leaving," Tompal spoke.

"You need some assistance in that venture?" Hayes pulled his leather coat back so Tompal could see the revolver, the star pinned to his shirt that read his title. "We was thinking this occasion might call for a few armed escorts and some shackles so you two won't hurt yourselves. It's rough country you're riding through. You're liable to encounter undesirables."

"Undesirables?" Tompal tittered. "The only kind we've encountered in our travels, Marshal, are good Christian types not unlike yourself, I'm sure."

"I fall short in a few areas. For example I take the Lord's name in vain quite often. The act fills me with quite a bit of joy, to tell you the truth. I've also been accused of imbibing on Sundays. In fact that's what I was aiming to do before y'all came along. I was going to get good and drunk and think up all the ways a man can take the Lord's name in vain. You've really put a damper on my day."

"We tend to have that effect on people."

"Nice looking folks like yourselves?"

"The Negro would resent your smugness. You're lucky he ain't here."

"And where did he get off to?"

Tompal stepped toward the wagon.

"If you'll just allow us, we'll be out yer hair. No one else has to die today. And let it be said that we didn't kill nobody. I conferred with the lady here and she swears the woman behind ye's the one that shot the man upstairs. You'll find him once we're on our way."

"The rumor is she can't talk. How'd she tell you all that?"

"We're real close, Marshal. Now if you don't mind, we need be headin' down the road."

"Don," Scoggins whispered.

"Yes, Deputy?"

"We don't have to do this."

"What?"

"You heard what they done across the Ohio. We could just let 'em go on. It ain't worth it."

Hayes shot his deputy an incendiary glance then returned his gaze to the fugitives.

Tompal took a step toward the horses. The mute followed.

"If either of them dirty whore's children take another step, Scoggins, shoot whichever one tickles your fancy."

"Excuse me?" Scoggins said.

"If that girl or that cocksucker standing before us takes another step, Deputy, I want you to shoot one of them. I don't particularly care which."

"When he shoots, Marshal," Tompal shouted, "should he shoot to kill or are you going to leave that part for improvisation as well?" Tompal burst into humorless laughter, raised the pump, and fired. Mud exploded in front of Hayes, who drew back and squatted behind the Tanner woman, grabbing her under her arms and pulling her toward Tompkins General Store.

Scoggins fired and missed. He chambered a round and fired again, hitting the mute's mare roped to the hitching post square in the eye.

Tompal returned fire. Craters appeared in the mud around Scoggins as if miniature cannonballs were landing. Scoggins stumbled circularly as the ground exploded around him and tripped in a fresh pothole, landing flat on his face in the mud.

While Tompal mounted the wagon, the mute drew a stiletto from her boot, cutting the leather that fixed the mules to the post.

She hopped onto the plank next to Tompal as he pulled the reins, shifting the wagon's course and pointing the mules north.

Hayes got the Tanner woman behind the horse trough. He stood, leveled his revolver and tried to get a bead as the killer took aim upon his deputy.

"Banks! I will shoot you dead." Hayes tried to thumb the hammer down but the sweat made his fingertip slip off the metal.

Tompal Banks pumped another round into the Colt and pulled the stock tight against his shoulder.

Hayes got the gun cocked and fired into the air.

He aimed again.

Tompal turned, flicked his wrists, raising the barrel, a muzzle flash distorting Hayes' view of the outlaw.

The shot hit the surface of the trough water. A wave of piss and horse spit blinded the frozen, cringing marshal.

Tompal got a bead on Hayes, who eyed his revolver now lying at the bottom of the trough.

The men locked eyes as resignation dawned over the marshal. He knew the killer had the drop on him.

Tompal lowered the Colt. He handed it to the mute who waved it at the crowd while he gathered up the reins, flicking his wrists again.

13

Hayes sent Scoggins for Doctor Hamilton. The marshal and Eliza Schultze carried the Tanner woman through the parlor into Eliza's bedroom. Hayes thought it best to keep her from the sight of whatever bloodshed awaited him on the second floor.

Eliza pulled off the woman's vomit- and blood-covered boots. Hayes propped a pillow under Geraldine Tanner's head then helped with the soiled pant legs that clung to her skin. He watched her shiver on the satin sheets while Eliza disappeared, returning with a damp washcloth. He left her to administer the care, taking the opportunity to sneak into the kitchen and take a few pulls off the boarding house bourbon to relieve the shakes.

It had been seventeen years since Don Hayes had been fired upon, since he truly believed he was going to die by the gun.

Hayes remembered the night.

He had carried the gutshot soldier from the valley below where the battle still raged. The man's name was Corey

Riley and he was from Mercy. When they were growing up, Corey, Hayes, and Wade would walk down to the Ohio to fish and hardly ever catch anything, usually quitting early to watch tugboats pass on the banks, talking about which girls were going to help them through the itching summer. Hayes was always saying how far he'd gotten with Laura Ludlow who lived next door or what the blonde and curvaceous Sally, who was married to Judge Barnett, had let him do to her.

He'd say it happened under the branches of a sycamore tree just south of Nicholson's, that he'd ran his hands up Sally's skirt while she took him in her mouth. He winked and told them that her other hair was blonde too. Hayes would give them all the details.

The stories Hayes made up were what got them through the first summer of their teen years.

In the darkness provided by the grove of trees they hid behind, Hayes ran his hands through Riley's bloody, blond hair as he drew his sidearm. He shoved the barrel of the cap and ball Colt under his dying friend's chin and pulled the trigger.

They were out of supplies and high in the Appalachians, miles away from any kind of medical attention, not that it would have mattered. Nothing could be done save the granting of a swift death.

Don Hayes had killed a man he had looked out for since they were little boys. He killed Corey Riley out of mercy.

Three days later, they got the news that the war was over.

Hayes snuck into the alley, removed his flask, swallowed the liquid courage, and headed upstairs to examine the second floor. The dead man slumped against the banister, a red wreath now encircling his thigh.

After five minutes, Hayes returned to Eliza's bedroom.

The furrowed brow that seemed a permanent fixture on the Tanner woman had straightened a bit. Her eyes eased as Eliza ran the washcloth in a circular motion along her forehead and cheeks.

"Did you fetch a bath for someone?" Hayes whispered to Eliza.

"What does that have to do with anything?" Eliza said.

"Lower your voice. You don't want to upset her."

"That killer had me bring up a bath."

"Was it for him?"

"He didn't say. Like I told you, he snapped at me earlier for prying."

So Banks does have some redeeming qualities, Hayes thought.

"Did you notice if Mr. Tanner had a gun on him when he checked in?"

The Tanner woman's jaw dropped to her chest and her eyes bulged out. Schultze noticed this and shot Hayes a hateful look. Her expression was answer enough.

"You said they all three shared a room?" Hayes changed the subject.

"They did."

"Which room?"

"Number One," Eliza said.

"Is that the first you come to? Right at the top of the stairs?"

"Yes."

"Mrs. Tanner," Hayes keeled by the bedside. "I need you to try to talk to me for a moment."

Tanner nodded, wild-eyed.

"Your husband's name was Clyde, correct?"

"Clyde," she said hoarsely.

"Well, I'm truly sorry about Clyde, ma'am. May I call you Geraldine?"

She nodded.

"Geraldine, you can call me Don. I need you to try and communicate as best you can what happened here today before Deputy Scoggins and I found you. Can you tell me about it?"

On the stairwell Hayes had found a .44 revolver that matched the caliber of shots that tore up the bathroom walls and the bedroom door on the opposite end of the hall, the same caliber that would produce a wound the size of the one that killed Clyde Tanner. Clyde had been shot on the inner right thigh, an odd place for a gunshot wound. Hayes couldn't figure out how anyone could have pulled that off, except Clyde himself or a person standing right next to him. The upper portion of his pant leg had caught fire. The gun would have had to have been shot inches from the cloth to produce a flame. There was also dirty water all over the bathroom floor from where someone had dove onto the tiles and knocked over the tub to avoid getting killed.

Hayes had briefly questioned Schultze as they walked outside to carry the woman in. The Tanners and Tompal's crew were the hotel's only guests. The couple had just checked in, their luggage still downstairs for Eliza to bring up. She was still in the process of doing so when the shooting began and she found shelter behind the front desk.

As Hayes figured it, Clyde would have been in a great position to have fired most of the shots. But his wife would have also. She had been upstairs with him when the shooting began, and given that she was covered in blood and the same vomit that was encrusted around his mouth, she'd probably been right by his side when he died. Most of the bullets had landed in Tompal's bedroom and the washroom where either Banks himself or one of his partners had taken a bath. The only shot coming from any other direction was the one that killed Clyde.

If Tompal or the girl or the missing Negro had killed this man they wouldn't have taken a risk and gotten in so close. They would have edged out into the hallway and taken a shot. And what reason would they have? Only one gun had been fired. That meant Tanner had either shot himself by accident or Geraldine had drawn the gun from his pants and it had gone off.

After that she must have shot the hell out of the hallway.

Walking downstairs to question the living witness, Hayes couldn't help thinking of what Tompal Banks had said to him on the boarding-house steps.

"And let it be said that we didn't kill nobody. I conferred with the lady here, and she swears the woman behind ye's the one shot the man upstairs..."

The Tanner woman stared at Hayes vacantly with no indication that she planned to answer his question.

"Geraldine," Hayes said. "What happened upstairs?"

"Tompal Banks killed my husband. He shot him down in cold blood while I stood there watching. Bring me my husband's killer, Marshal Hayes."

14

The wagon rolled and tumbled under a canopy of black cherry and shedding cypress high up the mountains north of Mercy. The mules had drunk deeply from the trough but had eaten only grass since West Virginia. The riders could not push them much farther or faster without putting their lives to risk.

They forged on until Tompal tightened his reins, the thick smell of smoke twitching his nostrils from somewhere behind them.

Tompal turned toward the mute for advice much as a general would his lieutenant.

"You smell that. Maybe there's someone can help us get these horses fed? Maybe show us a quick way into Ohio."

She nodded.

"Okay. Let's follow the scent."

He turned the mules around and steered them back the way they had come, then guided the wagon down a bank thick with paper leaves and fallen branches, hollowed out by creatures unseen. The smell grew stronger until Tompal halted the mules at the sight of black smoke kissing the treetops just beyond a drop-off in the bank.

He placed his arm around the muted and pointed toward the rising black cloud. As they drew closer they saw the mouth of a stone chimney barely over the treetops of the hollow below. They guided the wagon slowly down the slope, careful not to hit a rut and split an axle. Through the branches, a log cabin came into view. Dancing flames illuminated a standing figure in the far window.

A stone garden filled with withered rosebushes and empty dirt rows spread before the cabin. A brick path led to the front door, circling a miniature statue of the Blessed Virgin at the garden's center.

"It's tucked away," Tompal whispered as they hit level ground. "If there hadn't been a fire we woulda' passed right by."

The mute pointed to the small open stable to the left of the cabin, two mules hitched and sleeping within.

"We'll feed the mules, get our bearings and be on our way," Tompal said, more to himself than to the mute. "We didn't get no supper our own selves. I ain't even had a chance to wash up."

Tompal examined the mute, dirtier than she was before her bath.

"And no offense, baby child, but you could use a second going over."

Tompal dropped off the wagon and handed her the reins.

"We'll just keep heading northeast into Ohio. I'll get word to Falls City somehow. I can maybe get my man to send someone to Ohio to make the trade."

Tompal breathed in deeply, his indignation at the plan that had seemed so reasonable just that morning now crumbling before his very eyes. What had he expected.

That news of such a bloodbath wouldn't travel swiftly from one state to the next, as it had before through the Virginias. Their journey had been doomed the moment the mute set foot on those saloon steps in West Virginia.

He spat into dead leaves.

So what if he had let them down? There was no use crying about it now. Plans fell apart and people died and the only thing that mattered at the end of the day was the safety of this family he had put together, which this venture had compromised.

But at least she had remained unharmed.

He supposed he should thank something, perhaps, if nothing else, the Lenten moon, the clouds like gusted shadows, and the stars that had guided them this far. He was grateful that the precious child sitting on the wagon behind him still drew breath and could find it within herself to crack a smile across her face, that trail of tears that marked the first half of her life.

"I don't know about you, hon. But Kentucky can kiss my ass."

Tompal glanced at the cabin and the dead garden that separated him from its light.

"I'm gon' see what kind of people we're dealing with. I hope they're hospitable 'cause they got guests comin'."

Father Lance Garrison stood over a naked Selma Sheers. She lay askew on her stomach across the fake bear rug before the lit fireplace, her plentiful ebony backside arched toward the priest as he abused himself, his erect member aimed fixedly, the glorious final act.

She began to shake her ass as she had during their

courtship, strutting out of his quarters as she threw a knowing glance over her shoulder after bringing his morning coffee or the lunch she always prepared with extra love and care after the services that he dreaded more every week.

She was throwing such a glance and waving her behind one Sunday afternoon when he blurted it out, confiding in her that his faith in God was waning. He had said that he firmly believed if Jesus met one of these Catholics or one of Thurman's congregants, there would be no second coming.

Selma had told him right then that she loved him. She had ever since the church had taken her in when she was eleven years old, an orphan, her father a slave emancipated by John Avery, the owner of the largest thoroughbred ranch within a day's walking distance of Mercy.

Avery had, with the help of a young, idealistic Father Lance Garrison, gone through a profound psychic change, seeing the error of his worldly ways. He devoted himself to a life of poverty and humility, freeing all of his slaves and selling all of his land, the profits going to numerous charities. Avery had remained single and heirless throughout his life and therefore had no need to write a will, no children's futures to worry over. He allotted himself only a meager allowance and a clapboard shack in the woods south of Mercy. He would spend his days either in silent prayer or volunteering as Doctor Hamilton's assistant, nursing TB patients and the victims of other diseases most of the community deemed untouchable.

Then news of war came.

Avery, believing the institution of slavery to be both a societal and a spiritual blight, saw it as a sign, a personal calling from God.

Garrison pleaded with Avery not to go as he had pleaded

with the man not to sell all of his land, that freeing his slaves and committing himself to Christ and charitable acts was enough.

At first Avery agreed, however reluctantly, holding Garrison's opinion in high esteem for he considered the priest his spiritual advisor. The matter was dropped for almost the entire first half of the war. Then one night after mass, Avery approached the priest and informed him that he had enlisted in the Union Army and that was that. Avery compared the calling he felt to that which Garrison proclaimed to feel about the priesthood.

Garrison had never felt anything as intense as the fervor he saw in the eyes of John Avery. Selma's father, Henry, moved by Avery's awakening, joined the man in his enlistment and they'd marched off together.

It was ironic. A month after Henry and John's departure, a troop of rebels passed through Mercy, one of them badly wounded and in need of confession. Garrison provided the confession and the last rites to the dying rebel, struck for the first and only time in his life with a similar sentiment to that which Avery had described, stronger by far than that petty interest in western spirituality that had led him to the priesthood. He left Mercy with the rebels, providing solace and ministering to Avery's enemy, not because he agreed with slavery and secession but because they were children of God.

John Avery and Henry Sheers were slain somewhere near Cincinnati, leaving Selma an orphan and the town of Mercy short a merciful soul.

In all his charity and good will, Avery had neglected to think of the future of Selma, who, after only an infancy of freedom, had wound up a different kind of slave on the same land on which she had been born; she would be raised in a Catholic orphanage where Avery's farm once stood.

Garrison, knowing Selma's history, the tragedy of her father and his dear friend, made sure the girl was educated and treated with the utmost concern by the nuns who ran the orphanage. Around age fourteen she began to question the sisters' convictions, as well as her fellow housemates' blind acceptance in church teachings.

Selma would never stop with her questions no matter the punishment.

She would tell them that times were hard and God needed to either help his people out or change the rules so they could help themselves every once in a while.

When this insouciance arose, Selma was fifteen. To shield her from the wrong end of the sisters' yardsticks, Garrison made her his personal assistant in all matters and tutored her privately. And, unlike the sisters, he discussed these matters with her, honest in his general lack of an explanation.

She had been by his side for three years and how she had grown.

Selma giggled and said, "That's it," as the father finished, cascading her backside in what they had been moving toward all night.

The priest stumbled, his knees buckling, ready to give in and fall next to his lover when a tapping at the door sounded. Selma retreated down the back hallway to the bedroom to make decent for whatever company had arrived.

That was what bothered Garrison.

No one knew about this place.

He had no gun or knife save for cutting meat and those were too dull to be much harm to anyone.

It could be a weary traveler knocking, a soul in need of respite, Garrison's duty to give still. It was the only pleasure he took from being a priest anymore, helping those in need, seeing the relief on their faces. He was tired of the spiritual side of things. The church would rather have dead bodies than souls lost.

If this fearsome truth had not been clear to him before, it was made blatantly so when cardinals and archbishops from all over the state met to discuss their policy on gathering donations for the missionaries to disburse in the newly formed western territories.

Since the Missouri Compromise, Catholic churches within the Commonwealth had sent out and accepted gratefully all forms of charity for pioneers whose farms and livestock had been decimated by Apache attacks, the impoverished and disenfranchised, those who had gone out West seeking fortune and finding only hardship.

Garrison arrived at their conference uninvited, urging them to make canned goods first priority. He was escorted out of the archdiocese and told under no uncertain terms that he had just kissed any chance of upward mobility within the Catholic Church goodbye.

The conference yielded similar results to what, looking back, the now-embittered Garrison could have predicted. Only Bibles, crosses, or rosaries would be accepted now that the bureaucratic bludgeon had left its smite.

A base necessity like food did not make the list.

It was clear to him what spiritual matters could do to the minds of men. For the time being, the father was done with lofty pursuits of the ethereal. He had been just as guilty as the church fathers whose absurd beliefs and behavior now nauseated him, blindly accepting the belief that heaven was only to be had upon death and even then only if one had been baptized when Jesus himself said that the kingdom was among us.

He still loved shaking the hands of his parishioners as they left Holy Innocents after mass, rejuvenated. He loved holding them when they wept over their losses, offering counsel and whatever meager solace he could.

These were now his reasons for rising in the morning, not the promise of the hereafter or the prospect that intangible souls were at stake. He lived for the meat and bones of life matters.

If eternity yielded a God that didn't approve of what kept Garrison going, then to hell with Him. And if what stood beyond the cabin door meant him harm then he would have to stand by his creed in regards to such matters. He had always told himself and had said more than once to the Confederate troops he rode with, "Whatever will be, will be."

Garrison retrieved his robe from the leather sofa facing the fireplace and covered himself. He picked up his spectacles from the floor and put them on as he opened the door.

"Evenin'." The man grinned, holding his hat humbly to his breast, moonlight bouncing off his blue eyes and the long barrel of the blue steel .45 revolver which he used to scratch the side of his head of bushy black hair, flecks of white sprinkled throughout.

15

With the folded Union suit under his arm, Cody ran east
through the witchgrass between Mercy and the mountains
that formed a horseshoe around the town, taking account
of the thatched roofs over his shoulder that shrank smaller
every few moments, making certain no forces were giving
chase.

The gunshots that immediately followed his flight
brought hot tears to his eyes. He did not know what had
become of the girl and the killer he had ridden with since
that morning three years ago when the two had found him
beaten half to death in an Atlanta alley. His temporary
condition had been at the courtesy of some white boys
who suffered a mighty grim fate when they crossed paths
again six months later, Cody then fully recuperated and
not the least forgetful.

It had been over a white woman.

All Cody had done was open a door for her.

They told him during the beating that he was lucky they
didn't castrate him.

So when they gutted the hillbillies outside of Montgom-
ery, Cody made sure the one who'd done the taunting got

it last. As the boy evacuated his bowels at the sight of his eviscerated riding partners, Cody said to him, "You're lucky we didn't castrate y'all."

It was always either women or whiskey. While still trying to deal with the first, the latter, Cody had quit after his second jailing. Unfortunately, he'd been the last man standing in a Baltimore barroom brawl, the only Negro present, never a good thing.

He had been in trouble ever since he stuck his head out between his mama's legs and his eyes feasted on a Jackson plantation. He escaped with two other slaves at the age of thirteen. The other boys were promptly caught.

He ran now with his only possession clutched to the breast of his long johns, more than he had to his name when he'd fled that Jackson cage a lifetime ago. He sprinted until he spotted a ranch house in the distance, white with black shutters, a barn several yards behind.

He slowed down finally and caught his breath.

When Scoggins returned with the doctor, Hayes sent the deputy back out after Masterson with orders to have him report to the jail early and to wait for further instruction. He also told Scoggins to stop by the Newmyer place on his way back and have Christopher come to remove Clyde's body. Scoggins asked who was going to pay the undertaker's bill. Hayes told him to just get it done.

"Just tell him to get the body out of here," Hayes said. "I don't want him to build a casket for it. Tell him to bring his wagon and store it wherever he stores 'em until Geraldine's feeling better and decides what to do. If he makes a big to-do about whatever fee he's gonna charge, tell him we've given him several passes on bruisin' up his lovely wife and he should just consider this penance. I ain't got time to be worrying about Newmyer's bill. We've got to be getting after Banks."

Scoggins got back on his horse and headed out to Masterson's place.

Doctor Hamilton agreed to sit with Geraldine Tanner until he was confident her condition had stabilized. Eliza thanked him and went to the kitchen to fix herself and the patient some supper.

After talking to the doctor, the marshal turned his focus to Mayor Teague, patiently waiting in the late afternoon dark of Eliza's parlor to be briefed.

The men sat in red leather sofa chairs that faced one another, the mayor nodding calmly at Hayes as if to tell him this situation needed no unnecessary drama. Teague offered to have some men who did work for the town remove the dead mare in the morning. The same men would fix Tompkins' trough. To make matters easier, Tompkins and Schultze would not be billed.

Hayes thanked the mayor for this and also for insisting that the swarthy Walton stay home on this one.

"He owes me, you could say," Teague said.

"Does he?"

"I've looked the other way on so many of that man's backroom deals that I've put my own soul at risk. I'd say the least he can do is allow me to do my duties for once without him breathing hot air down the back of my neck."

At times, the mayor made Hayes his surrogate confessor.

The marshal never complained. He did not ask for specifics and the mayor rarely offered.

"I used to wish I had money and power and such,"

Hayes said. "I suppose every young man does. Now I see how many problems you people have and I'd just as soon drink the cheap shit."

"The elite drink wine, Hayes." The mayor gave the marshal a half grin.

"There you have it. I never did go for that whore piss."

"It tastes all right, but the hangovers are wretched. You definitely wish you'd had whiskey when you wake."

"Amen."

"You don't think Banks shot Tanner?"

"It sure don't look that way."

"What are you going to do?"

The mayor stared through thin drapes out the window at Thurman preaching on the front steps to his fellow worshipers and the whores from Barmore's and anyone else who stopped to listen, his vigil for the victim resting within.

"Me and Scoggins are goin' to ride north into the mountains. That's where Banks and the girl headed."

"Even though you believe they committed no crime here."

"They're still wanted in West Virginia."

"If you bring 'em back, you know what Thurman will do. You remember the hell he raised over the Duncan trial. He wanted the hanging to take place the day after the arrest. You think this'll be any different?"

"What do you suggest?"

"Let them go."

"Shit."

"I'm serious. Ride off into the woods, camp for the night, come back and say you couldn't find them. They'll be Ohio's problem."

"Jesus, John. You can't give him that kind of power.

I've got to try to stop them before they cross into another state and hurt somebody else. Just 'cause they didn't do no harm in our town don't mean they ain't a threat to society."

"That isn't part of your job. Your job is to defend Mercy and uphold its laws. That's it."

"What's gotten into you?"

"I don't know why I didn't see it, Hayes. But it hadn't fully hit me how powerful that prick Thurman had become until this afternoon. What I'm trying to say to you is that if something happens…if he starts trouble over this, he's got friends in high places now. It's not going to be like it was last year with him alone on the court steps or outside the jail screaming like a lunatic. He's got sway because of the sheer size of his congregation and because…"

"Because what?"

"Because he's got money and he's got a certain councilman in his pocket."

"Walton?"

"I didn't even need to drop a name."

"Are you givin' me an order?"

"Just think about it."

"I've thought about it and I've made my decision."

"Are you ready for what will follow that? You could have a full-scale riot on your hands."

"You can't let those people dictate the law."

"They have the numbers."

"And we have to be able to count on what reasonable citizens there are left to do the right thing if the occasion presents itself."

"I could lose the town to them if you bring those two in."

"It sounds like you've already lost it, Mayor," he said before turning and walking out of the room without another word.

As Hayes stepped from the parlor to the foyer he heard the kitchen door being gently pulled shut.

He wondered how much Eliza had heard of his conversation with Teague.

The marshal left the boarding house to meet his deputy at the jail.

Hayes and Scoggins reloaded their rifles and revolvers, hung full ammunition belts across their hips, strapped extra ones to their horses, and were mountain-bound by nightfall, the north star their only compass.

Most of the congregants had dispersed to their respective homes and shanties on the edge of town and by the river, but only after being promised solemnly by Thurman that they would be sent for if more news on the situation came his way.

God's only true ministry in Mercy would be prepared this time.

The four members of the repentant Mills gang rode back to the family farm having assured Thurman that they would bring back with them whatever was left of their infamous arsenal.

He was alone now in the alley between Tompkins General Store and The Brass Ass, Thad Barmore's sinful enterprise now in full swing. Thurman watched the emaciated Doctor Hamilton speak with Eliza Schultze in the boarding-house doorway across Central, no doubt leaving her instructions on how to care for her ward. Hamilton tipped his hat, bowed, and headed down Central. Eliza closed the door.

Thurman waited for Hamilton to turn down Twelfth

Street, half running now, eager to get back to his office where morphine awaited. If Hamilton only knew the elation our Savior could bring, perhaps the good doctor would be cured of his addiction.

A matter for another time. Thurman stepped ever so lightly onto the muddy thoroughfare toward the shelter where there lay a prospective and promising convert.

16

Neither had given struggle.

The owner of the cabin, the gray-haired, bespectacled priest they had seen when they first rode into Mercy, greeting his parishioners on the front steps of Holy Innocents, had stood aside, the door ajar, and held his arm outstretched, offering his unexpected guest the interior of his weekend retreat. Tompal glanced over his shoulder at the mute and motioned toward the stable with his revolver, indicating for her to hitch up the mules.

He asked the priest if there was feed in the stables and the priest quietly said, "Yes."

Garrison had been surprisingly forward, introducing them to his Negro wench Selma, offering refreshments in the form of French bread, beef stew, and smoked sausage.

"We brought too much," Garrison explained. "I suppose we were so excited about our time together that we let appetites run rampant."

"We been ridin' and ran right out of provisions. I'd be in y' alls debt if one of you'd fix me up a plate."

The mute slapped Tompal's thigh, furrowing her brow when he turned to look at her.

"Sorry," he said to her, then turned back to Garrison. "She'll take some too. We thank ye."

"I take it you could use something to drink."

"Anything you got."

"We have water and wine."

"How 'bout a little of both?"

"What happened there?" Selma pointed to the bite marks on the mute's wrist.

"We ran into some undesirables in the Virginias."

"I'm sorry to hear that," Garrison said.

Tompal kept the revolver on his lap. Mention was not made of it, nor its implications, that Selma and the priest were hostages.

Garrison had been whispering to her when he brought her into the living room, Tompal still not sure about the man, ready to shoot him if he came out armed.

But the situation had remained amicable.

The mute chewed savagely at her bread, sopping up the leftover stew from the tin plate on her lap.

Tompal drank straight from the canteen, glancing back and forth between the barely clothed Negro girl and the holy man, only mildly curious about their arrangement.

He then eyed the dying embers in the fireplace still giving off too much smoke for his liking.

Garrison followed his gaze.

"I take it gathering more wood for the fire wouldn't be a friendly gesture at this point."

Tompal nodded agreement.

"Would you like me to snuff them out?"

"They'll be dead soon enough."

"True."

Tompal said to the priest, "We'd just like to get our bearings, get our mules tended to and we'll be out your way. I'm truly sorry 'bout this."

"Why are you sorry?" Garrison motioned with his hand as if swatting away a fly.

"Just bargin' in on y'all like this. I'm sure you weren't plannin' on a coupla strangers to come ridin' down that slope and interruptin' your evenin'."

"We're all strangers at some point. With that in mind, how could I turn you away? I may be the one on the other side of that door someday."

"This ain't the normal welcome we receive."

"I'm not the normal welcoming committee, I suppose."

"Well, that's a fuckin' relief."

17

The rotting carcasses of two long dead mules lay between the house and the stock tank. Erastus Mills had unloaded upon them with a .44 a month ago. He had killed dozens of the animals in his life. In all instances, the patriarch had accused them of being stubborn before opening fire. It was never out of mercy. Ike had been ten when he'd seen his first mule shot before his very eyes by his father and remembered the instance well as the gang locked their horses in the ramshackle corral a few yards to the side of the rickety windmill. Ike held his breath as they walked past the two corpses, maggots swarming in and out of their open ribcages.

"When are one y'all gon' clear out them stubborn sumabitches?" Erastus barked. "I didn't kill 'em so I'd have to look upon 'em the rest of my days."

"I'll get right on it." Deke slapped Roy on the shoulder and they rushed to the mule closest to the porch. Roy reached for its legs while Deke went for its neck.

"You gonna give us a hand, Ike?" Roy asked.

"I didn't mean do it now" Erastus said. "Do it in the mornin'. We got to get back to town."

"Those mules ain't going nowhere." Ike snorted as he

stepped over one of the bodies toward the sagging porch.

Lantern in hand, Ike led the way down the rotten wooden steps to the family cellar, refusing to assist his invalid father. Erastus had used the ride home to browbeat his son. He'd also employed a myriad of bodily functions and venereal diseases to describe Ike's mother who'd died in labor. This was to be expected on a Sunday. Erastus was prone to fits of rage after keeping his speech pure for too long a period.

Luckily, the old man was easier to ignore than he had been before a stroke interrupted his ravaging of that poor retarded girl he insisted on having the first turn at. His slurred and monotonous speech, mixed with the clapping of the horses' hooves, allowed Ike to write the old man's incessant verbal abuse off as just another sound of the trail home, as inconsequential as a whippoorwill's lonesome song or a cock crowing somewhere barely within earshot.

"I assist ye in yer tyranny and I assist ye in yer goddamn holy rollin'," Ike said as he manipulated his way, feeling with his free hand the mud-wet cobblestone walls that encapsulated the narrow passage.

The hall opened into a workroom that had gone neglected since they'd bought the place with stolen Union funds. Ike turned to his father before breaching the barrier, his bearded, skeletal face angered in the dim light of the lantern, resembling some gnashing demon.

"Now, I'm assisting yer tyranny in the name of fuckin' holy rollin' and ye still run me down every chance ye get, old man. I don't know why I still do this to myself."

Erastus, shrunken and hairless, stood between Roy and Deke, their elbows locked to support their crippled figurehead.

"If ye knew what was best fer dis famly, I couldda gon' 'head an' died by now."

"What?"

"Ye'd have us all dead if I left it to ye. Now move."

Erastus twirled his long, white mane as he nodded toward the workroom.

"Ain't no God that would ever forgive the things we done, Erastus. You especially, you vicious bastard."

"Ike, come on now," Deke said.

"What's a matter, Deke? You getting tired of holdin' the old skeleton upright?"

"This ain't necessary," Roy said. "We need to be headin' back to town."

"Shut up, ye mouth breathers. Both ye'd lick his arthritic testes if he took the notion."

"This ain't about no God," Erastus said.

"Marcus Thurman might disagree with you."

"He'll see soon 'nough. I got 'im right where I want 'im."

"I'm tired of being God's obedient little nigger every Sunday just like I'm tired of being yours every day of the damned week."

"Yer just doing yer part. Suck it up."

"And I'm tired of being humiliated. It'd be nice to know, just for once, what pride felt like."

"Let's jus' git' dem' guns and be on our way. I'm tard o' lookin' atchye."

<h1 style="text-align:center">18</h1>

Cody buttoned the dark blue trousers around his hips, heaving at the tight fit, the only light to guide him the nightfall creeping through the cracks in the barn roof above, slightly lighter than the interior dark.

The legs of the federal uniform barely touched his ankle tops and the sleeves of the coat only came a few inches past his elbows. He had to accept the suit for its function rather than its gallantry, the night cold of late fall enwrapping him even in the barn insulated by haystacks and thick oak.

He sat to pull his boots back on and was gripping the leather on the second when the barn door creaked open. A rotund, balding man stumbled in dressed in a fine black broadcloth coat, a floral vest underneath, double-barreled shotgun in his grips. Cody shot up, kicking his foot into the boot as he limped toward the rear doors.

The man, obviously drunk, leveled the shotgun at Cody, cocking both barrels.

Cody halted at the sound, raising his arms in supplication as he turned to face his captor.

"I knew if I searched long enough I'd find another nigger waitin' somewhere on my property to deep cock my woman," the man said.

"You got the wrong nigger," Cody said.

"What are you wearin'?" The man stumbled closer to Cody.

"I just found it. It ain't mine."

"Are those Union blues?"

"Shit."

"This is ironic. A Union nigger defrocking my wife. Of all the women you could have picked, you picked a Bostonian's wife. Why didn't you choose one of these hillbillies to cuckold? What did I ever do to you? It is because of families like mine that you niggers are free. There would be no white pussy for you if it weren't for my half of the Mason-Dixon. Where is the gratitude?"

"I don't know you or your wife, mister."

"I don't know why I expected anything different. South of Illinois and Ohio, they're all niggers."

"I just needed a place to change clothes. All I had on was my long johns."

"I bet. I bet you were getting good and hard waiting for Bea's deep cunt to wrap its lips around that cock of yours. Let me see that thing, boy. I bet it's something."

"I'm gonna' tell you the truth, sir. I'm on the run from the law and I used your barn here as a momentary hidin' place while things died down in Mercy. I had no idea there was somethin' goin' on between a man o' my color and your woman. This is one big clusta' fuck's all it is."

"Just the kind of story a horny nigger would come up with. You don't even think enough of me to get imaginative with your lies. Well, I'll tell you what. I think you may just be a case for Marshal Hayes to deal with. Come on."

The man pointed the shotgun toward the barn door behind him and stood aside for Cody to walk in front.

Cody moved toward the man as he had been directed.

"Wait. I forgot."

The man aimed the gun at Cody's crotch.

"I want to see it."

"This really ain't necessary."

"Now, nigger!"

Cody unbuttoned the trousers and let them drop.

The red hue that had consumed the man's face lightened.

"It's not that bad," Walton said.

He looked genuinely let down. "What's all the fuss about? Everyone talks about how big they are. That looks about normal to me."

The man lowered the gun, motioning to the door again.

"Pull up your britches, man. You're still going to jail."

Cody bent down and grabbed hold of his trousers.

"Sorry to disappoint you," Cody mumbled.

"Move!"

"Geraldine." Eliza Schultze leaned over her ward, sleepless since the doctor's exit.

"Yes," Geraldine said in a voice vacant and hushed.

"I wouldn't normally bother you, honey. But given that you ain't sleepin' I figured you might could use some company. Do you remember the man who found you this afternoon in the street?"

"The preacher?"

"Yes. He's a reverend. But he's more than that. He's like some sort of prophet. He's been touched by the Lord's hand. He's got himself a big congregation. He's made miracles out of men that most would have been written off as lost a long time ago. I lost of a lot of faith when my husband died in the war, Geraldine. I am here to tell you that the reverend has restored every bit of it."

Eliza ran her fingers through Geraldine's short, raven hair.

"Unlike the other men that have come to me, he didn't once take advantage of my loneliness. He comforted me with something so much greater than the pleasures of the flesh. I still fall behind, Geraldine. But Christ forgives."

Geraldine Tanner fell to weeping. "I been lost a long time."

"I was too, baby."

"I've done some bad things."

"No worse than most of the reverend's congregants, I'm sure."

"Can you call for the reverend?"

"Oh, darlin'. He's already here."

19

They broke from the trail where the wagon tracks faded a mile up the north mountain, riding up a leafy bank and dismounting in the center of a sparse grove of black cherry trees.

Both lawmen drank plentifully from their canteens. Hayes drew his away from his lips first, wiping his mouth with his coat sleeve.

"The tracks just stopped. It don't make no sense."

"It's night and all we got is a half moon and two lanterns to light our way."

"They broke from the trail. That's the only thing it could be. We just need to get our bearings and figure out which way they headed. East or west. I couldn't rightly tell."

"They had a head start, Hayes. We didn't leave Mercy until two hours after they did. You know how many night creatures could have compromised their tracks since they passed through here? Or even other travelers? There are people that live in these mountains. A lot of the ironworkers who don't want to pay the cost of living in town reside on this mountain here."

The marshal ignored Scoggins. "Maybe they invaded one of them poor boy's houses."

"They could have gone anywhere, Hayes! And here we are lookin' more like fools than we did this afternoon. I done told you we should have waited until mornin'."

"When they'll be halfway to Cincinnati."

"It ain't our fight. We done our job, Hayes. We ran 'em off."

Hayes stood at the tree line that overlooked the trail.

"I don't see what stake you got in this," Scoggins said. "They killed a man that wasn't even a Mercy citizen. I ain't tryin' to be insensitive or nothin'. But thems the facts. Can you please explain to me why it's so urgent that we bring these two back that we rode off in the middle of the night into this mountain of dark? We got a lot going against us. We cain't see shit and they got the high ground. Can you tell me why it's worth putting our lives in that kind of jeopardy?"

Hayes breathed steam into the dark blue light that crept through the trees.

"You're right."

"What?"

"We shouldn't have come."

"That's a first."

"When you're right, you're right."

"You ain't never told me I was right before."

"That's 'cause usually you ain't right."

Hayes took another pull off of his canteen.

"What now?" Scoggins said.

Hayes placed his canteen in his saddlebag.

"We're going home. I let Tompal Banks get under my skin and in doing so I put both our lives to risk. I'm sorry,

Scoggins. I truly am."

"I don't understand. We rode up here because you're mad at him? Why? He could have killed you and he didn't."

Hayes mounted his horse and glanced down at Scoggins for a moment and then looked away.

"I guess that's exactly why I'm so put out with him. I feel like he was makin' fun of me or somethin'. Like he was playin' with me."

Scoggins grabbed hold of his saddle and placed his right boot in the stirrup. "Maybe he just didn't want to kill you."

"Let's just go home, Scoggins. I said I was wrong. Ain't that enough?"

"Seriously. Maybe he ain't as cold-blooded a bastard as that woman made him out to be. That's a possibility, ain't it?"

"It just ain't fair. How come Tompal Banks gets a mute and I get stuck with a man who can't keep his mouth shut to save his life?"

The rustling of leaves from somewhere on the other side of the trail halted Scoggins' retort. Both men turned to the twilight creeping between the trees.

"Stay saddled," Hayes whispered.

Hayes quietly let himself down from the horse, squatting as he crept over and leaned against a tree trunk to get a look.

The wagon, Tompal at the reins and the mute beside him, ascended the bank not fifteen yards down on the other side of the trail awash in moonlight.

"It's them." Hayes turned to Scoggins. "They turned off the trail. That's why the tracks stopped. How come I didn't think of that?"

"'Cause it don't make no sense that they'd turn around."

"Kill them lanterns."

"Shit," Scoggins said.

He shook his head, frustrated. The deputy had just become confident that the workday had finally ended.

"Do it, goddamnit."

"Okay. All right."

Scoggins put them out while Hayes had himself another look.

"They're headed our way."

Hayes tiptoed back to his horse, grabbed the reins, leading it to a tree close by. He wrapped the leather around the trunk.

"Scoggins, I'm gonna double back on foot, come up behind 'em. I want you to count to twenty. Say 'Mississippi' between each number. Then ride out onto the trail in front of them. Have your Winchester out, ready to shoot. You understand me?"

"We was just ready to go home."

"That was then. This is now."

"You want me to go face to face with the two of 'em by myself?"

"Don't worry. I'm gonna knock that son of bitch right off that wagon. I ain't gonna give him the chance to draw. We just gotta time it right."

"There's quite a bit of room for error."

"Not as much as you might think. Remember, I done this kinda thing before."

"I woulda enlisted myself if it weren't for my back. I'd a been useless to you boys for at least two weeks at the start of winter."

"You were a teenager, Scoggins. You're telling me you had back problems when you were seventeen?"

"I've always had 'em. For two weeks I'm useless. You know that."

"As opposed to the other eleven and half months of the year."

"If we're going to do this, let's do it. I'm tired of getting grief from you."

"Suits me just fine."

Hayes finished tying up his horse, drew his Winchester from his saddle sheath and bent his head low as he headed along the bank south.

Tompal guided the wagon at a medium pace along the trail where, not long before, the smoke had led them to the priest's cabin and the strangers' kindness therein.

A cluster of clouds drifted between them and the moon that guided their path, and before Tompal could form the prediction, a light drizzle fell upon them.

The mute turned up her collar and pulled her derby low.

"We couldn't expect that spell of good luck to last, I suppose," he said. "Shit."

She snickered, agreeing with him.

The rain hitting the leaves on the trail and the banks below and above them made a ticking sound akin to a clock's hand sounding off the seconds.

They had gone less than a dozen yards when the incessant ticking was overcome by the crackling sound of footsteps flattening the dead dry leaves, somewhere closing in behind the wagon on Tompal's side.

Tompal pulled on the reins to slow down the team. He stood halfway, one hand on the cover for support when the Mercy marshal he had let live appeared on the wagon beside him, jumping up from the trail and getting hold of the cover rim with a quickness that left the outlaw reeling.

Tompal sat back, aghast at the sight of the lawman now standing beside him, holding a Winchester by the barrel.

Hayes swung the rifle in an upward arch, knocking Tompal off the wagon and onto the side of the trail, leaving him behind in the dust.

Hayes flipped the Winchester around but by the time he got it leveled the mute had dropped off the wagon and shot down the bank out of sight. He grabbed the reins and gave them a tug, stopping the trotting mules in their tracks just as Scoggins' horse ambled down the upper bank.

"What happened?" Scoggins aimed his Winchester in every direction.

"Come on." Hayes jumped off the wagon and waved for his deputy to follow him, walking back to where Tompal Banks had fallen.

The killer was right where Hayes had left him, bracing himself against the rising slope with one hand, the other holding the side of his face now bleeding where the brunt of the barrel stock had landed.

"You all right?" Hayes said.

"I'll make it." Tompal sounded drunk.

Hayes struck him again, this time in the ribs.

Tompal tumbled over, clutching his belly, and a wheezing sound escaped his teeth as he bit his lower lip.

"Jesus, Hayes," Scoggins said, free of his saddle now and standing just behind the marshal, bridle in hand.

"The other one disappeared down into the brush yonder." Hayes pointed. "I'm going after her. You watch him."

"What do I do if you don't get back? I mean if it starts to look like you ain't comin' back?"

"It's a girl. A goddamn teenage girl, Scoggins."

"Did ye get a look at her?"

"Yes. What's your point?"

"She ain't like any girl I've ever seen."

"If I don't get back in due time you get him back to Mercy and lock him up." Hayes cocked the lever of the Winchester. "And keep Thurman as far away from that jail as humanly possible even if you have to pistol-whip the holy bastard."

Hayes shifted his boots and headed down the bank after the girl, adjusting with every step down, careful not to lose footing. He could see himself stumbling, doubling over, rolling head over heels straight into some tree trunk, cracking his head open and dying like a fool, an appropriate end after his defeat in front of the entire town today. He could have put an end to all of this shit and shot Tompal Banks dead. Instead he wound up covered in trough water, unarmed and helpless, naked at last before his community.

Now they knew what he was, a no-account loser just like the vagrants he rolled, worse than the pig iron workers he jailed weekly. For despite their vices and infidelities, at least there was some fight left in them. He had never heard of one losing his wife and child to an Arkansan drummer.

Not a man among them would let his family, the only thing he could truly count on, slide so slowly through his hands as Hayes had upon his return from battle. It was like his father had always said, "We either hang together or we hang separately."

Ruminating on such matters in his trek down the bank, Hayes failed to take notice of the thick, fallen branch lodged between two cypress trees. In his thoughtlessness, he'd picked up some speed and when his boot hit the obstruction, the Winchester flew from his grip. His hat shot off his head, skipping down the bank after the Winchester. He threw his hands out to brace himself for the fall and as he landed, winced as bolts of hot pain shot through his palms.

The toe of his boot caught onto the log and halted his descent. He rolled over and lay on his back, one leg resting on the dead branch. When he moved his foot, he howled. He rested it back on the log, knowing a few of his toes were broken, and possibly worse. He stared at the branches above, the leaves sparse now that fall was upon the mountain.

He wept, a flood of tears unlike anything he had experienced in his adulthood breaking loose from some cavern within that he had spent two decades damming.

He apologized to his wife and son. He told them he had done the best he could but it just wasn't good enough. He told them everything. He confessed to the mercy killing. He said that he was so young and dumb when he signed on to go kill all those men. And for what? The only reason he could find was the illusion of glory now gratefully broken.

He closed his eyes and wiped his face dry, pulling his foot from the log as he sat up. He looked ahead and just beyond the log, within reaching distance, the mute squatted, studying him like a hawk would its prey before descending for the kill. Her hat was still low, obscuring her eyes.

"How long you been standin' there?"

She cocked her head over her shoulder as her mouth

curved upward into a smirk.

"Can you answer me somehow?"

She nodded.

"Did you see me fall?"

She nodded.

"Did you hear everything I said?"

She stood, nodding the same answer as before. She stepped over the log and stood above him as he slipped the rawhide thong off his revolver's hammer.

She pounced just as he freed it from the holster, squatting again, her derby knocked aside by the swiftness of her motion. She grabbed a handful of his hair, pulling his head back as she drew a Bowie knife from her boot.

The blade was a bristle from his throat when he pressed the barrel to her chin.

"Back off, you hellish bitch, or I'll decorate that face another color," Hayes said.

She drew the blade back just barely.

Hayes kicked at the branch, scooting out from under her.

They stood in unison.

She tossed the Bowie knife down the bank past him.

"And the stiletto," he said.

The smirk turned into a sneer as she knelt and drew the other knife from her boot, tossing it in the same direction as her hat and the Bowie.

He kept the revolver sighted on her forehead as he stepped over the branch, his hand and trigger finger both steady as brass bookends.

They were both on level ground now.

It was the first time Hayes had seen her without the hat. She gazed at him with big brown eyes glowing of such innocence he could nearly forget that she had just tried to slit his throat.

The eyes drew him in for a moment. Without the hat pulled low to hide them, she looked like a different girl, the markings the only similarity, and they in no way hindered this vision's natural beauty.

He blinked to snap himself out of the spell she had cast simply by looking at him.

"Turn around and start back up the way you came," Hayes said.

She stared for another moment, her gaze betraying not a trace of the feral wrath he had seen when she attacked him.

The faintest smile crossed her lips, and as soon as it had formed was lost to its audience as she turned to do as her captor had instructed.

20

Deputy Wade Masterson lit the lantern and hung it on a coffin nail stuck in the wall above the gun rack. Aside from being the youngest arbiter of the law in Mercy, he was also the cleanest and most presentable. He wore the finest tailored suits, usually navy or black, combed his sandy blond hair every time he removed his hat, and drank only moderately. He was a picture of youth and respectability and never heard the end of it from Hayes and Scoggins.

He was content in his lone vigil. There had been no fights reported between drunken men from Nicholson's or complaints of vagrants stinking up the stairwells of city dwellers.

He decided to treat himself. He found the bottle in the marshal's top left hand drawer, and, using one of the tin cups left from coffee trips to Schultze's Boarding House, poured himself a taste.

He sipped at his whiskey, wishing luck to the riders, Hayes and Scoggins, the derelict replacements for the brothers he'd lost in the war. Scoggins had introduced him to the wonders of loose women while Hayes continued to do his best to offset the damage. Breaking up fights and rolling drifters was a small price to pay for the time he got to spend with the two.

Hayes had showed up to the house two days after being elected marshal asking Masterson for a moment alone with his mother. As Wade closed the door, he spied the Confederate kneeling by the tubercular, bedridden Emma Masterson, her skin as thin around her bones as candle wax close to a flame.

Wade knew Hayes was promising Emma he would look after her boy. He had made the woman the same promise when Wade and Hayes had enlisted together as teenagers. Emma had already lost two sons to the Confederate cause and Hayes' word meant little to her at the time. But when the two came back alive, she credited her son's survival to Hayes and from then on treated the man like a saint. Wade was offered the job of deputy the day after the future marshal's visit, two weeks before Emma died. He was honored by the gesture even though he knew it was not based on merit. He gladly accepted.

He was fighting his eyes, leaning back in Hayes' chair when the first knock of the evening came to the bolted front door.

Masterson stood, drawing his Colt as he approached.

"Who is it?"

"It's Councilman Walton. I have a prisoner."

In the councilman's attempt to hide being drunk, his careful pacing of words and pronunciation, he gave himself away.

"You have a prisoner?"

He said it so lackadaisically, as if he himself wore a deputy's star. Masterson shook his head, holstered his piece and unbolted the door.

The rain had stopped, leaving the street muddier than usual. The rooftops dripped onto the porches causing eerie, discordant sounds to echo back and forth across Lexington Avenue.

An astonishingly tall Negro with a head of thick white curly hair dressed in Union blues at least three sizes too small stood on the porch, the councilman behind him on the bottom step, a double-barreled shotgun resting on his forearm.

A group on horseback watched from across the street. Masterson squinted, his eyes adjusting to the night.

Erastus Mills sat beside his son, Ike, who held the reins of the mule leading the wagon. Beside them in formation, Deke Hagstaff, Roy Thompson and the halfwit Meriweather twins, all former hellraisers turned holy rollers thanks to the noble Reverend Thurman, sat saddled and ready to raise hell again.

Masterson glanced at the wanted poster on Scoggins' desk. The whole town would by now know the description of the third man at the murder scene today, one that matched explicitly the Negro standing on the porch before Masterson. And it would be only a matter of time before the reverend heard word of his capture.

"Walton, you think maybe you might've been little less conspicuous about bringin' your captive in?" Masterson said.

"What would you suggest, Deputy? Have one of my daughters keep an eye on this big-cocked grizzly while I come and fetch you? Or should I say medium?"

The councilman giggled and lightly elbowed the Negro in the back.

Masterson did not understand the reference.

"Do you know who this man is, Walton? The last thing we need is the whole town knowing he's jailed."

"He said something about being wanted."

"He is. You hear about what happened at the boarding house today?"

"Yes. But the mayor in all his limp-dicked wisdom felt it proper I be left off the cleanup detail. How was I to know this nigger was involved in that horse fuck?"

"You still should have the good sense not to bring a Negro to the Mercy jail dressed in Union blues. You should've sent for me. This is just askin' for trouble."

"Look, Deputy, I wanted this animal off of my property and in the hands of the proper authorities before he could do any more damage to the women of our community."

"Fucker's silly," the Negro whispered to Masterson.

Walton drew back the stock of his shotgun and rapped the Negro across the head with it. The Negro grunted as his knees gave and he collapsed, Masterson catching him as he fell. The deputy allowed the prisoner to drop to his knees, rubbing at the back of his head and cursing under his breath.

Masterson drew his revolver and stared at the councilman, snake-eyed.

"Go home now, Walton, or I'm going to be fillin' two of them cells."

"Are you threatening me?"

"No. I'm giving you a chance to sleep in your own bed for the night, you no good, drunk sumbitch."

Walton stepped down onto the mud, his jaw agape as he held the deputy's stare.

"The marshal will be hearing about this, Wade."

"I'll tell him myself. We'll have a nice laugh over it.

Somethin' to make the time pass while we're waitin' for one 'a them workers from the factory to show the community his gratitude toward that benevolent father-in-law of yours. You know, the same one made a councilman out of ye."

"This isn't the last you'll hear of this."

"Piss off, ye walleyed puss lover."

Masterson leaned down to help the Negro to his feet.

21

"Are you repentant of your sins?"

"Yes, Reverend, and they are many."

Geraldine Tanner, up to her knees in the muddy waters along the banks of the Ohio, wept still, Thurman beside her.

His ministry gathered on the riverbed holding torches to light the ceremony, an occasion to celebrate another soul saved from the plagues of an earthly life.

Eliza Schultze had gotten the word out to the first few congregants and it had spread like wildfire from there. Any children were to be left at home this time. Thurman had not told her why, but she had an idea. Eliza had informed the reverend of the conversation she'd overheard between the mayor and the marshal, conveying that today's killing was not the first the three she'd housed were responsible for. They were wanted in West Virginia for similar crimes even though Hayes had possessed the audacity to suggest that the poor innocent Mrs. Tanner might have been the one that shot her husband, not the disfigured mute, the nigger, or the foulmouthed white man.

It did not surprise Thurman. These sinners were completely inept in carrying out the laws of God. Only a man pure of heart such as himself with the backing of his faithful flock could make that law a reality.

Thurman had thanked Eliza and after ministering to Geraldine and securing her agreement to be baptized, sent the proprietress to spread word among the congregants to meet at the river's edge.

The Mills gang had yet to return but word had gotten to the reverend that the Meriweather twins had taken it upon themselves to ride out to the farm and notify Ike and Erastus of the baptism.

"Do you forsake the life you lead before Christ, those who would tempt you from His grace and the worldly traps which would cause you to stray from the path He has laid out for you?"

"Yes. Yes."

"Do you accept God as your Father before all, His word as written in the Bible your only instruction, more holy than the laws of man?"

"I do, Reverend."

"Do you accept Jesus Christ as your Lord and Savior?"

"Yes, yes. I'm ready."

Without another word, Thurman pinched Geraldine's nose, placed his other hand between her shoulder blades, backpedaled a step, and immersed her upper half in the moonlit waters, immediately pulling her back upright.

As he lifted her, he shifted his hand, placing his palms on her shoulders, turning her so he could see the change.

She beamed with light. The water cascaded down her face, blackened by the sins it had removed. She was now beautified in Thurman's eyes. He placed his lips to her forehead then turned to face his flock, a satisfied man.

He smiled wide at the sight of the Mills' wagon rolling down the bank, the halfwit twins in tow.

The second knock came not an hour after Walton left, drunk and undignified.

The Negro had been a placid prisoner, far less maintenance than the usual fair at the Mercy jail. He had passed out upon hitting the cot in the corner cell, the one Marshal Hayes fancied for sleeping one off.

Masterson got up, drew his pistol, and held it against the small of his back.

As he unbolted the latch and opened the door a crack the discordant dripping wafted in from the street. Standing on the porch was the reverend. The red rash that had only been visible on his cheek for the past few years now formed blotches from his scalp on down to his neck. Masterson had seen such markings before, the unmistakable symptoms of incurable syphilis. The reverend probably caught it in his years prior to conversion, when he traveled the south, a drunken, raping, and pillaging rebel soldier. It was a time that he often referenced in his self-flagellating fire and brimstone sermons that he delivered on street corners and in his tent on the edge of town. Masterson marveled over the reverend's ever growing congregation made up predominantly of miscreants and the mentally ill. He supposed they were the only people who could be expected to follow such a hollow man.

"I am to understand you caught one of the transgressors."

"What are you talking about, Thurman?"

"The three who shot up Eliza's place."

"I don't know what concern that is of yours."

"We can't let that kind of abomination pass through these parts unheeded. The souls of the tortured must be spoken for, Masterson. You know what those three done?"

"I'm not at liberty to discuss this with you right now."

"The woman whose husband they killed. They also shot down his brother, a sheriff in West Virginia, after murdering three other men in cold blood and committing a robbery."

"They ain't even been tried yet. Don't know what they done until a judge or a jury hears the case. Witnesses have to be brought in. It's a process. You see, Reverend, this is why we don't discuss certain things out in the open. Rumors start circulatin' and who knows what's liable to be spread. We..."

"My grandfather used to tell me about how when Virginia owned this state they'd have to send for permission to retaliate against Indian attacks. By the time the messenger came back with a 'yea' or a 'nay' the Indians were long gone. The women and children had been slaughtered and scalped, the stations pillaged. Should we really be waiting for permission to do what we know is right in our hearts?"

"Thurman. There's a way of doing things."

"And then there's justice."

"That's what I was referrin' to."

"I'm talking about the kind that comes from on high, my son."

"And you think you know best how to execute it?"

"The Lord works through us."

"Does He, now?"

"And the wages of sin are death."

"What about your sinners? The ones that gather by the river."

"They've repented. These three have not. And I seriously doubt they have plans to."

"I'm at a loss here, Reverend. Maybe you should just come back and speak to Marshal Hayes tomorrow."

"Last year when Margaret Chiles was raped and killed and that man walked around carrying her head under his arm like it was a pumpkin he had carved up into a jack-o'-lantern, like something he was right proud of, you didn't do anything about that, either."

"You're exaggeratin' a tad bit, Reverend. All we know is that we found him with it, not that he did what you said, walking around with it, holding it up for all to see. If that had happened there would've been some more witnesses and you'd have had your speedy trial."

"You forced the family of the victim into prolonged strife. There is no trial but the one the Lord administers. You know the grief it brought my congregation having him sleeping not a mile from where their children lay."

"You didn't have a congregation back then. In fact, if it weren't for the show you put on because of that murder you might not have one now. If I didn't know you as a man of God I might mistake you for a politician in the making."

"Not a politician. An aspiring fisher of men like the Savior. Nothing more, nothing less. But you are unnecessarily hindering those aspirations, lawman."

"We don't even have all the facts yet, Thurman. Were you there? I wasn't. Most what you've said is secondhand or even thirdhand information. All we know is that there's a wanted poster with their faces on it and they were present at a murder scene today."

"Geraldine Tanner witnessed Tompal Banks kill her

husband. I've talked to her."

"You should leave that woman alone."

"I was offering her solace."

"If you want to finish this discussion, you should come back when the marshal's in. Hayes and Scoggins didn't have a lot of time to fill me in on what happened. They just told me about the murder and the shootout and showed me the poster. The truth is, even if ten people saw him do it, this country has a constitution and it states that we have to proceed with due process. That means we have to have a trial and bring in the witnesses and gather all the facts before we hang them. It's the best way. Better men than us have relied upon it. We don't know which one of them pulled the trigger. One of them could have been sleeping at the time. If that's the case we couldn't rightly hang that person unless they had helped plan the murder. And there's also the crimes they committed in the Virginias. You see, that complicates matters quite a bit. So, just be patient, will you. Let us and the judges do our jobs. That's what the town pays us for."

"The one who killed the Chiles Girl, he wasn't human, Masterson. He was something else. You think he was the same as you or me?"

"You'll just have to talk to the marshal when he gets back. Marshal Hayes and Deputy Scoggins are out looking for the other two right now. If they succeed in apprehending them I imagine it'll be a nightmare in regards to where the trial is held and where the hangings take place, if in fact hangings are in order. Now why don't you go on home? It's late."

"I can't sleep knowing what's coming. I don't see how you can either, Deputy."

"I need to get back to work."

"So do I."

"I appreciate your concern, Reverend."

Masterson shut the door, now sweating as hard as the syphilitic lunatic on the porch beyond.

PART THREE

Of Whores and Holy Men

22

They spotted the torch fires a third of a mile down the mountain, a full block of Central Avenue ahead of them aglow in the midnight dark.

The shackled prisoners had remained complacent in their fates on the slow ride back to Mercy, the deputy behind them with his Winchester resting on his lap, the bridle of Hayes' horse tied to his own. Farther back, the marshal steered the wagon that carried the hundred-plus guns he and Scoggins had discovered in Tompal's wagon.

Tompal had refused to answer any questions about their cargo and Hayes did not press the matter, tired from his tussle with the mute and the long day behind him.

The only other inquiry he made concerned the mute. Scoggins requested her name, to which Tompal replied laughingly, "Why don't you ask her?"

No more was said between the lawmen and the killers until they came upon Mercy.

Four blocks past the city limits he signaled to Scoggins to cut over to Central at the alley just before the boarding house. They parked the wagon in the alley, dismounted, and cowered behind the lawmens' horses and the trough in front of Schultze's. Scoggins kept his rifle trained on the outlaws' backs. They watched the mob crowding the front of the Cap n' Ball Saloon two blocks down, across the thoroughfare from where they hid. Thurman stood on the porch, spitting and waving his hands about, describing to his denizens the path that had brought the Negro hanging from the rafters beside him to such an awful end.

Tompal removed his hat at the sight of Cody, his face bloody and torn from where they must have dragged him kicking and screaming to die in this land he bewailed.

The mute leaned against the trough, turning to meet eyes with the marshal for the first time since her capture on the bank, a benign and pleading expression softening her features, asking him to do something.

Hayes averted his gaze down Central Avenue.

The new gaslights that would normally brighten the windows of Schultze's and the other businesses were out. Even the Western Union office was closed. The lines on the posts surrounding the building were cut and its front windows shattered.

There would be no way to send for help, to relay to the world outside of Mercy the horror that had befallen the town.

The congregation wept and screamed as the reverend preached on. The Meriweather twins, Otis and Lyle, both halfwits suspected of raping cattle two counties over, swung the dead Negro between them like children would a tetherball.

"They will see justice when they come!" Thurman held up an index finger. "They will see what a God-loving and God-fearing community does to they who follow the Devil's path. For there may be two paths, family, but there is only one way. The end of times is upon us. A battle must be fought and sides must be chosen." Thurman pointed to the swinging man. "He chose the wrong side."

The crowd roared, pitchforks and axes rising, lauding Thurman.

"Stay here and keep them quiet. I'm going to head over to the jail, see about Masterson," Hayes said to Scoggins.

The crowd bore scythes, double-barreled shotguns, axes, Winchesters and other assorted implements of destruction, swinging the blades in the air and firing at the heavens as Thurman paused to enjoy the bedlam he had created in the name of Christ.

"How many you think there are?" Scoggins said.

Hayes made a preliminary headcount.

"At least forty."

Hayes rose from behind the trough.

"Keep that rifle trained on them. I'm going to see about Masterson."

"Hayes," Scoggins said.

But Hayes had already disappeared into the shadows of the alley.

Hayes squatted, his hat in his hands.

Masterson lay on his back in the cell furthest from the door where Hayes had begun his day. The deputy had been shot at close range, his face a mess of muscle, bone and brain matter.

"You fought every step of the way, didn't you?" Hayes said. "They had to back ye up to a wall to get you. I wish you'd just let them have him. I know it makes me a son of a bitch sayin' it. But now you're both dead. Do you see my point?"

Hayes fell back against the cell bars, turning his face away from his dead friend. He composed himself and used the bars to pull his body upright.

He stepped back into the main room of the jail.

The two desks had been upturned, the one closest to the door now lying on the floor. The gun rack was empty. The boxes of shells kept on the shelves underneath missing.

"I ain't one to talk," Hayes said. "I never did the smart thing. The thing I'm about to do now probably ain't what Councilman Walton would advise. I'm gonna go kill me a holy man."

He stopped at the two Masterson had taken with him, both ironworkers Hayes had grown accustomed to hosting at the jail for assault and public drunkenness—until Thurman's Baptist ministry had offered them salvation, reformation, and redemption.

One was sprawled halfway through the open door. The other lay face up in the mud with his boots on the porch, dead eyes staring vacantly at the empty sky.

If that was what salvation looked like, Thurman could keep it.

"Man's got himself a faithful flock," Tompal said after Scoggins briefly relayed the history of Reverend Thurman, from his street preaching to his flourishing tent ministry to the disenfranchised and the former outlaw element of Mercy.

"I don't get why they didn't just hang him on the jail porch?" Scoggins said.

"Central's the busiest street." Hayes appeared from the alley and squatted between the deputy and his prisoners.

"More people will see this way and word'll spread faster. The only thing on Lexington is the jail and the courthouse. Shit. If they'd hung him a street over we could just cut him down before anyone sat eyes on him."

"What about Wade?"

"The Negro was in the jail house. I don't know if Wade went out and found him or if someone brought him in. They broke down the door to get to him. Wade killed two of 'em in the process."

"The Negro had a name. It was Cody Williams," Tompal said.

"So did the man who died defending him. His name was Wade Masterson."

"Well I didn't know the man, Marshal," Tompal said. "Sounds like he had some grit though, taking a few of 'em with him like that. That's the way to go when you got your back to the wall."

"Any sign of Teague or Walton or any of our other honorable city officials that might be interested in a crisis like this?" Hayes said.

"No. No one's showed up. I think Barmore must have closed down when he saw what was goin' on. Normally at this hour the whores are still at it."

"I can't believe this."

"Thurman's just been preachin' away," Scoggins said. "I guess he's on a roll."

"That killin' must've really brought the spirit out in him," Tompal said.

Hayes stood.

"Get back down," Scoggins whispered. "They'll see you."

"I don't care," Hayes said. "The circus has taken over the town, Scoggins, and I don't find it the least bit amusing."

Hayes limped toward the congregation.

"Shit," Scoggins said glancing back and forth between the two prisoners, Hayes' figure growing smaller as it began to blend with the crowd.

"You think he's coming back?" Tompal spat.

"Hush yer mouth."

"There's a whole lot of them and only one of him."

"He'll be back. He's a war hero, the marshal. Don't worry, he'll be back."

"Okay. I just wanted to hear you say that. I feel better now. You feel better?"

He tugged at the mute's coat, the fires of the congregants dancing in her eyes as she looked on.

"Paul writes in his Epistle to the Ephesians 'For because of these things cometh the wrath of God upon the children of disobedience.'"

Hayes stepped behind the crowd of onlookers, his revolver held to the small of his back, his hat low.

"This Union nigger who rained sorrow and strife upon all he came into contact with is now in hell serving his eternal sentence. Besides that, nothing else is relevant or consequential about him. He is but an example, brothers and sisters, of what form the payment for the wages of sin can take if repentance is not prompt."

"Enough," Hayes shouted.

"Who said that?" Thurman said.

Those surrounding Hayes moved away, making clear to Thurman the source of interruption.

"This man has been judged, Marshal, by a court higher than that which you serve. God's people have spoken."

"Well, I just talked to God and He wanted me to tell these people that you're batshit crazy. The Lord has decided that killing people might be best left up to Him from now on, Him and the city court of Mercy as far as you're concerned, Thurman. So why don't you step down from there. As for the rest of y'all, go home."

The crowd just stared, their eyes filled with sureness in their God's instructions through Thurman's word.

"You have no hold on them. What were you thinking even coming around here, Hayes?"

"Reverend. In the past twenty-four hours I've been lied to. I've been shot at. I've had my position in this community taken into question. And I've seen five dead bodies, all of which can be attributed to parties present." Tompal glanced at Geraldine Tanner standing at the edge of the crowd next to Eliza Schultze, who stared coldly back at the marshal.

"One of them was my friend," Hayes said, turning back to Thurman. "To answer your question, I wasn't thinking. I'm tired. I'm angry. And if you don't get down off of that porch I'm going to kill you where you stand."

Hayes brought up his pistol.

"Anyone move and your beloved prophet dies like a river dog," Hayes yelled at the crowd. Panicked now that he had drawn down on their leader, they took aim with their weapons accurately in his direction.

"Leave him be," Thurman said.

"You killed an officer of the law."

"He chose his side."

23

Scoggins could not believe his eyes, the marshal raising his gun at Thurman in the midst of the armed crowd.

"He just killed himself," Tompal said. "Probably us too, unless we get out of here."

"Shut up."

"Here's what you need to do now, Deputy. You need to unlock these chains and walk away. Consider us no longer your concern. I saw you whisper to the marshal this morning when I gave y'all a chance to let us ride out. You knew it was the right thing to do. Considering what we're dealing with now I can't imagine your opinion on the matter has changed much."

"You don't know shit about me, Banks."

"Really? What was you sayin' to him then?"

"What if I were to just give you up to them? You ever think about that? Just feed you right to those sick sons of bitches. You think I want to die saving you? The same man that tried to kill me this morning, and made me look a fool in front of the whole town."

"I wasn't trying to kill you, Scoggins. I was aiming low just to throw ye off."

"I still don't see no reason not to give ye up?"

"To be perfectly honest, me neither."

Scoggins grabbed Tompal by his coat and lifted him to standing.

"What are you doin'?" Tompal said.

Scoggins handed Tompal the key to his shackles.

"Chain yerself to that hitchin' post." Scoggins took a step back, throwing the mute a key and ordering her to chain herself to the flagpole a few yards in front of the boarding house, keeping his rifle trained on the pair as they worked, yelling for them to hurry up.

"I'm going to assist the marshal," Scoggins said.

"We're helpless like this, Scoggins," Tompal said. "Think about it."

Tompal nodded to the mute.

"She's in plain sight. All they gotta to do is turn around."

"Marshal Hayes and I are going to deal with the situation down yonder on the thoroughfare and then we'll come back for you. Just don't make no noise."

"You're killing us, Scoggins."

"I don't think all the marshal's faculties are with him. I'm gonna try to pull him away from that crowd before he gets himself kilt. Then, like I said, we'll come back for ye."

"What if you don't, Scoggins?"

"I'd say at that point, I ain't gonna be too concerned about what becomes of the two of ye."

Scoggins traipsed toward Hayes and the torches and contorted faces surrounding him.

Tompal did not call after him, his silence now their only facade.

* * *

A face in the back of the congregation turned to Tompal and the mute.

"Here we go." Tompal knew it was over.

They had been recognized.

"Reverend," a voice from the crowd shouted. "The other two."

"What?" the reverend said.

"The other two," a woman screamed, running past Scoggins toward the boarding house, pointing to Tompal Banks and the mute, chained and helpless in the twilight.

Hayes felt something grab at his arm. He fired into the crowd around him twice and ran.

Scoggins stopped at the mob's edge when he heard the shots. He saw Hayes backing away, Colt extended.

The congregation moved around them, heading toward the two chained in front of Schultze's.

The mute kicked at the thin flagpole, saw it was no use, then straddled it.

"Don't forget about me," Tompal said.

Like a wild animal, she shimmied up the pole that stood as tall as the boarding house. She reached the tip, holding tight with one arm as she pulled the flag to the wood, then lifted her shackles over. She dropped back down to the street right as one of the congregants was upon Tompal, a woman with a raised scythe.

She fell, arms out, pulled her shackles around the woman's neck and twisted her wrists until she heard the snap.

The woman dropped to the dirt limp as a doll.

She picked up the scythe by its two handles and in one sling of the blade decapitated the two men with axes that had been creeping up behind her.

* * *

The batwing doors of The Brass Ass parted before Scoggins.

The grandeur of Barmore's bar lost some of its luster when unlit by the gilded gaslights. The chandelier above looked like broken glass rather than crystal, and no music came from the grand piano so carefully positioned in the center of the gambling hall.

Several of the whores Scoggins frequented were on their hands and knees huddled under the roulette tables. Barmore was nowhere in sight, perhaps hiding behind the expensive bar to Scoggins' left.

"Barmore," Scoggins yelled above the sounds of gunfire and pandemonium behind him.

The pimp peeked his head from behind the bar and was opening his mouth to speak when a chunk of the chandelier above shattered. Barmore disappeared again and Scoggins covered his head to avoid the falling shards of silver and crystal.

Scoggins turned to face the double doors. Backpedaling, he fired as quickly as he could eject shells.

The congregants formed a half-circle around them. Tompal grabbed the mute's arm and they ducked under the wagon's cover.

"Start loading," he yelled, throwing over his shoulder the lid of the first crate he came to.

He shoved two revolvers into his belt then pulled out a Spencer. He found the proper shells in one of the niches between the guns and began loading.

On her knees beside him the mute pushed rounds into a

Schofield. She had it loaded within seconds, snapping it shut and firing out the open flaps of the wagon.

Tompal ran out the other side, grabbing the mules' reins, wailing men and women all around him. He fired into the crowd, dropped a few of them, then lowered the Spencer as he watched the first mule consumed by the mass of Baptists, their axes and sling blades tearing the animal to pieces before his very eyes.

Tompal backed under the cover and screamed for the mute to run.

His revolver clicked dry.

Hayes twirled it so the butt was extended, and began swinging, knocking teeth loose and smashing in the noses of anyone who came near.

Eliza Schultze's face appeared from the orgiastic mass flooding past him, a cap and ball Colt in her right hand. She stood out of reach from him so his makeshift club could not harm her.

"You too, huh?" he said.

Hayes threw his pistol aside and spat at the proprietress.

"This is forever, Marshal," she said.

"What?"

"What he's given me is forever. It ain't like you men that come and go, dyin' and lying like it don't mean nothin'."

"If this is what forever costs, Eliza, I ain't payin'."

"You just don't have no faith, Hayes," Eliza cocked the revolver.

Hayes shut his eyes and gritted his teeth, preparing for what was coming.

<h1 style="text-align:center">24</h1>

The mute pressed her boot into the proprietress's back next to the curved blade embedded deep between the dead woman's shoulder blades, wiggling the handles and widening the wound until the scythe came loose, falling backwards as the farm tool gave up its bite.

Tompal bent down and wrung free the revolver from Eliza Schultze's hand, then stood upright and snapped his fingers at Marshal Hayes, who stared agape at the body lying facedown in the mud before him, yet to be convinced of his own survival.

"Hey," Tompal said. "Look behind ye."

The bulk of the mob that had besieged the chained outlaws and then flooded the alley where the wagon was parked had turned back toward the saloon. They marched in formation toward the lawman and the two killers.

"Come on," Tompal said.

Tompal turned toward the saloon to see two cross-eyed men in overalls. Standing beside them was a young girl of no more than twenty in a floral dress with a black bruise that had swelled her eye shut. All held shotguns and blocked the way south on Central.

Hayes eyed Otis and Lyle Meriweather.

The twins and the girl made no move and did not speak.

"Lacey," Hayes said. "Don't you think Christopher might be wondering where you're at?"

Hayes felt a little guilty using Lacey's drunk husband to get to her, and also wondered if the louse might be present in the murdering crowd.

"He's passed out drunk, Marshal," Lacey said.

As usual, Hayes thought.

It made sense, considering the breaking-down her no-account husband subjected her to daily. She was the type Thurman preyed upon. Hayes wished he had been keeping tabs on who was making trips down to the river, on who had been seen under Thurman's tent.

"I'm sorry, Don," Lacey said.

"Don't apologize t' 'im," Otis said to her. "He's protectin' dem two."

"Lacey you don't have to do this," Hayes said.

She lowered the shotgun.

Otis stepped back and punched Lacey in the back of the head. She dropped her gun and buckled at the knees. He caught her by her hair and pulled her up, pressing the barrel of the shotgun to her cheek.

Tompal glanced over his shoulder, the marching congregants not a block away.

He looked at the mute and then at Hayes, nodding slightly.

Hayes grabbed hold of the Spencer in Tompal's left hand as the killer raised Eliza's cap and ball, holding down the trigger as he tanned the hammer with the flat of his hand four times in quick succession. Otis stumbled back, clutching his neck to stop the arterial spray, letting go of

Lacey's hair now matted by his blood.

The mute dropped the scythe. She drew the Schofield from her belt, steadying the gun with both hands as she fired, shattering Lyle's wrist before he could get the shotgun to chest level. The halfwit had not yet touched his ruined joint, nor opened his mouth to scream, when the shot that killed him barked from the stolen Spencer in the hands of Don Hayes.

They stepped over the two bodies, Hayes helping Lacey to her feet.

She tore herself free of his grip and sprinted toward First Street, jumping onto the boarding house porch to avoid the oncoming traffic of the congregants Tompal and the mute had narrowly escaped.

Reverend Thurman was now joined on the saloon porch by four men, three of them armed with rifles.

Hayes recognized Thurman's personal guard as the Mills gang. Erastus, steadying himself with a cane, pulled from a long leather sheath attached to his belt a Confederate cavalry saber. The younger men around Thurman levered rounds into their chambers and began taking aim on their helpless quarry. The alleys around the saloon and the stables next door were blocked off by more members of Riverside Redeemer.

"The Brass Ass!" Hayes screamed, waving the Spencer at the sign hanging over the darkened building on the eastern side of Central.

They had no other choice—the congregants who'd killed Tompal's mule came screaming like banshees at their heels.

* * *

Kneeling at the bottom steps and aiming through the banister rails, Scoggins almost shot the marshal when he entered Barmore's foyer, shattering the glass encasing a nude portrait of Venus.

Tompal took aim at Scoggins, recognized the deputy, then lowered his piece.

"Where you been?" Hayes asked Scoggins as he reloaded, leaning against the front desk.

"Surviving," Scoggins said, approaching Hayes, the outlaws and the whores gathering in the midst of the gambling hall's ruins.

"A lot of folks in that business." Tompal stared out the window across the street at his friend dangling. "Not many of them making a profit."

"Well, I'm trying my fucking luck," Scoggins said. "Ye alright?" He patted Hayes on the shoulder. The marshal brushed off the deputy's hand.

"Where were you, Scoggins?"

"Survivin'," Tompal answered for him.

"Shut up," Scoggins snapped.

"Were you in here seeing if your fuckin' strategy worked, Scoggins, while we were out there catchin' hell? Seeing if maybe the whores gave it up to you for free once they smelled Eliza Schultze's juices on ye? I ought to take you out back and shoot you, ye useless—"

"Don't talk about her like that," Scoggins said.

Hayes slapped his deputy across the face. Scoggins drew his hand to his cheek and lowered his head as the marshal talked on.

"I'll speak of her any damn way I please. It seems your precious proprietress has gone and joined Thurman's holy ranks. Were you aware of that, Scoggins? She just tried to shoot me out there and you know who had to save my ass since you weren't backing me?"

Scoggins glanced over the marshal's shoulder at the mute and Tompal.

"Aw hell."

"While we're on the subject." Hayes lowered his voice, deescalating. "I got some potentially upsetting news for you."

"She dead?"

"I'm afraid so."

"Well, it probably woulda only been a matter of time before she was trying to get me to accompany her to them services."

"Sounds like it worked out for the best." Tompal stepped back to the saloon doors, peering out the cracks. "Now, nobody panic."

Tompal stuck his revolver through the crack between the doors and fired two shots.

The men behind him staggered back, cupping their ears,

"What'd you do that for?" Scoggins said.

"A few of 'em were edgin' toward the steps. Needed to let 'em know we got our eyes open."

Barmore stepped from behind the bar. His slicked-back hair and mustache both glistened. He was a short, stout man with a goatee and bright emerald eyes that glinted with a salesman's confidence, a spark that dwindled slightly on this particular day. He shook as he approached the hall's center, the sawed-off shotgun he held bringing him no comfort.

"What about the back?" Hayes screamed at the whore man. "Can anyone get in from the back?"

"No. There's only one door to the alley and I slid the

board into the brace and locked it shut.”

“You think it’ll hold.”

“It’s steel. It’ll hold.”

“You better be right.”

“Marshal.” His voice broke. “I should have been out there to warn you. I remained in the street for as long as I could, but it nearly drove me crazy. Their torches and the guns and his maddening fuckin’ voice that would not cease, them swinging back and forth that dead man. I can’t believe what’s happened, Marshal.”

“We saw the lights from the torches. We had plenty of warning,” Hayes said.

“Yeah,” Tompal said. “We could’ve turned right around and been halfway to West Virginia by now but Hayes had to play hero. If you had to walk in the middle of that crowd of raving lunatics you could have at least freed us of our shackles.”

“What I meant to say,” Barmore continued, “was that Mayor Teague left me a message for you before he rode off to—”

The sound of breaking glass stopped him in mid-sentence and succeeded immediately by an axe whizzing through the room and embedding itself into the bartop. A large, bearded man wearing denim overalls with no shirt underneath appeared outside the broken glass of the northern window. He picked up one of the rocking chairs Barmore used for advertising purposes; two or three whores would at all times be seated on the porch, breasts shaking as they swayed, fanning themselves, cooing catcalls to men passing by.

The man outside began knocking out what was left of the window.

Tompal stood before the breaking glass and stuck the barrel of the late Eliza's cap and ball between the jagged edges, firing twice into the man's chest. He pulled the trigger a third time but the gun clicked dry.

Tompal tossed it out onto the porch as the man fell back onto the planks, lifeless. He drew one of the .45 revolvers from the wagon and began loading shells from his coat pocket as more of them ascended Barmore's porch.

Barmore and the lawmen surrounded the window, bracing themselves on either side while Tompal finished loading, firing at the oncoming believers through cracks in the glass.

The mute covered the southern window, aiming high as she shot small holes through the pane. She spaced her shots, getting beads on the dark figures that were replaced quickly and with impunity when one fell at the firing line.

Tompal appeared across the window from her.

"They got the other one covered," he yelled, holding the .45 with both hands as he aimed.

The mute broke down the Schofield and began reloading. Where a grouping of shots had collected and weakened the glass, a beefy hand broke through the window, grabbing her by her hair. She dropped the gun, shells scattering across the hardwood floor as the hand pulled her head against the broken glass that cut into her scalp.

Tompal stepped closer to her.

A shot pierced the window in front of him, causing him to halt. Another sent him back to his side. He returned fire and was ready to try to cross again when a brunette whore with a beauty mark on her left cheek stepped beside the mute, hitching up her dress to reveal a holster beneath her garter belt. She drew a silver Webley Revolver, shoved the gun through the hole the hand had formed, and fired twice.

The hand went limp, let go of the mute, and withdrew back into the writhing mass of flesh and fire outside.

The crowd finally flooded from the porch onto Central, scattering in every direction. They disappeared into the alleys across the street leaving behind seven badly trampled corpses riddled with gunshots.

It seemed the defenders of The Brass Ass had secured for themselves a momentary reprieve.

Silence filled the gambling hall, the survivors staring at one another, dumbfounded at the absurdity that had befallen them.

The mute tugged on Tompal's coat sleeve.

"What?"

She held out her hands upturned, her palms open. In one was the Schofield, in the other a single shell.

She mouthed the word "wagon."

"Shit," Hayes said. "So that's how she tells him things."

"She could talk once," Tompal said to Hayes. "She knows how to move her lips. She's a mute because her tongue was cut out. She's not a halfwit." Tompal turned back to her, nodding over his shoulder at the marshal. "Your condition is to your benefit when dealing with assholes."

"What was she telling you?" Barmore said.

"The guns," Tompal said. "They got our guns now."

<h1 style="text-align:center">25</h1>

Thad Barmore told the marshal how he had been the one to ride out to John Teague's house to wake the mayor and tell him that they had stormed the jail. Barmore had watched them drag the Negro across central to the saloon. Norman Wells, its proprietor, begged Thurman to leave his property until Otis Meriweather slapped him repeatedly, at which point the bar owner walked dejectedly down Central Avenue until he disappeared into the night.

While Otis and Lyle prepared the noose for the Negro, Abe Tremont and Eliza Schultze had tried to gain entrance to the Western Union office but the door was locked. They had then broken one of the windows out with the stocks of their rifles and crawled in. Moments later, Taylor Guthrie, the late-night telegraph operator, was thrown through the other window. While Taylor gathered himself up and limped off in the same direction as Norman Wells, Abe, and Eliza appeared on the office's roof to get closer to the telegraph lines so they could shoot them loose.

Barmore had been a staunch opponent to any power Reverend Thurman might secure, a man who would love to see The Brass Ass shut down and its whores turned into scripture-quoting sewing sisters.

The customers of The Brass Ass, as well as the piano player, the bartender, and the bouncers, had all ran for their lives. The whores would've done the same if they'd had somewhere else to go.

Moved to action not just by the sheer barbarity, but by the notion that Thurman was causing him to lose business, Barmore went door to door, from the apartment that Tompkins kept above his hardware store to the livery on First Street where the drivers were known to stay up drinking and playing cards. No doors opened to him, no answers to his incessant rapping.

He had been left standing alone in the streets of Mercy. It was as if the town had cleared out at the sight of the mob, gone to stay with relatives in the hills or maybe simply refusing to answer until the macabre events had subsided. Then he crossed the alley over to the jail and found Masterson, stumbling back outside to wretch off the side of the porch.

Upon Barmore's immediate arrival, Mayor Teague had acted a bit awkward toward the man, considering his station in the community. But once the nature of the visit was explained, Teague was all business, thanking the whoremaster for being such an upstanding citizen, dressing and retrieving his dragoon and lantern for the journey back to town.

The brothel owner and the mayor then rode back to Mercy proper side by side. They arrived in front of the saloon just in time to see Otis Meriweather, the ceremonies surrogate hangman, kick the whiskey barrel, on which they'd forced Cody to stand, out from under him.

Teague's face had gone pale at the sight of the swinging

man. He turned his horse around and headed back toward the jail. Barmore followed without being asked. Teague personally examined the wreckage inside the jail and the corpse of the deputy, then told Barmore they were going to pay the city's favorite councilman a visit.

Standing in the darkness of the farmhouse's study, Teague ordered Walton to get dressed. The Bostonian was half awake and draped in a black silk robe, sipping whiskey from a tumbler. When the councilman asked why, Teague told him they were going to ride to Ashland, where there was a state militia brigade.

Walton laughed in his face.

"Let's cut our losses," the councilman said.

"What?" the mayor had said.

"Feed them the other two. They're going to be hanged anyway. If the marshal does in fact apprehend them, let's spare the community any more collateral damage and get it over with. Who cares if it's Thurman's minions who do the killing? They have more manpower now than the town does. The militia won't make it in time, Teague."

"That zealot that you are helping to bribe into power just killed one of our deputies. Why are you not more concerned? You worried you'll have to refund him the money you took if he winds up in jail? Or maybe you're thinking he'll take you down with him?"

"I'm telling you that crusading at this point will only cause more bloodshed."

"You are a cowardly son of a bitch and I'd beat you to death right now if your wife and daughters weren't downstairs."

"Have you lost your mind?"

Teague punched Walton in the jaw, sending him spinning across the study. Walton grabbed at one of the book-shelves that aligned the walls, struggling to keep himself from collapsing. The shelf broke and Walton fell onto his back, a fourteen-volume leather-bound set of law books tumbling down after him.

Outside Walton's farmhouse, Teague mounted his horse and ordered Barmore to tell his wife what had happened and to take their twelve-year-old son, James, to be with her sister just outside Mercy County, to wait there until he sent for her. He also entrusted to Barmore the important task of informing the marshal promptly upon his return that the state militia was being summoned.

"Like I told you before," Barmore said to the marshal, speaking in a flurry of words. "I'm sorry for not getting word to you sooner. I had no idea what they would do next out there."

"What's important is help's on the way."

"For all I knew they'd string me up right next to the nigger for being a flesh peddler," Barmore said. "The reverend has made it abundantly clear to all that will listen that The Brass Ass is one of Satan's many stations in Mercy and that it's the citizens' Christian duty to see to its destruction. If these fine women didn't provide the men of this community with sufficient alleviation, you and Scoggins would have hell to deal with. They'd be like savages, raping and pillaging to assuage those urges for which we offer cheap relief."

"Too cheap if you ask me," the whore sporting the Webley said.

"Not now, Wanda," Barmore said.

"You leave us only enough to fuel our pride with the watered down whiskey you serve, ye cheap bastard," Wanda yelled.

Barmore backhanded Wanda. She staggered, dropping the Webley, both hands going to her lip where he'd struck her.

The mute appeared behind the whore man and placed the barrel of the Schofield to the back of his head.

"I wouldn't do that again if I were you," Tompal said. "At least not as long as baby child there's around to see."

The mute lowered the Schofield and retrieved the Webley from the floor, handing it to Wanda. Wanda removed a hand from her bleeding lip which already showed some swelling.

Wanda accepted the gun and threw her arms around the mute, bringing her in tight then letting her go. She stepped up to the pimp and slapped him across the face then went to stand behind Tompal and Scoggins, who watched the thoroughfare from the southern window for activity.

"How long ago did Teague set out for Ashland?" Hayes said to Barmore.

"I don't know." Barmore rubbed his cheek. "It must have been an hour ago."

"That means at best he won't be back until tomorrow evenin'," Scoggins said. "Shit."

"We don't know that," Hayes said. "This is what them militia boys are there for."

"I thought they was there for Indian raids," Scoggins said.

"Well, we ain't had a large scale Indian raid in this state in over fifty years," Hayes said. "I'm willing to bet them boys got time to spare."

"How far away's Ashland from here?" Tompal said.

"About thirty miles south," Scoggins said.

"That's at least a day on horseback if you don't push it."

"I'm betting he's pushing it," Hayes said.

"So if the horse survives it and this mayor of yours makes it and he's able to assemble the cavalry in a timely manner, when exactly can we expect to be seeing our rescuers?" Tompal said.

"At best, tomorrow night. At worst, Monday."

Tompal laughed, shaking his head and turning away from the milieu.

"Remind me again why I don't break off and run?"

"Because there's at least fifty armed men and women outside who want your blood. And make no mistake, as we speak they are blocking every path to escape."

"That's what I thought."

26

He should have brought a second horse.

Teague knew better than to push Powder this hard but he had to make up for the time he'd wasted on Walton. Said to be one of the best thoroughbreds in Kentucky, even Powder had his limits. If the horse died he would steal one if he had to. He would find a cabin up the bank from the river trail and make off with whatever animal he found on the property. He would take note of the location and reimburse the owner when all this was over.

He steered Powder down to the silt and dismounted, allowing the horse to rest and drink from the river while he sipped from his canteen. He laid down on the silt and fought his eyes. He had at least twenty more miles to go and it was a safe bet the lawmen had returned to Mercy by now. He could not know what hell had filled the streets of his city.

He sat up, adjusting his eyes to the dark.

Three figures approached from the south.

Teague rushed to his feet, backing toward Powder. He retrieved his dragoon from the saddlebag and turned to see three children, two boys and a girl. The boys looked to be thirteen or fourteen, a few years older than the girl. They all wore rags. The girl's dress was torn at the fringes, her hair disheveled. The boys wore dirtied dress shirts too large for them, suspenders holding up their baggy pants.

The children stared at him with callousness that would in a perfect world remain reserved for old men.

Teague hid the dragoon at the small of his back, flashing the children a smile.

"Hello," he said.

The children continued looking at him impassively.

"I was just taking a rest. I've got a long journey ahead." He couldn't even tell if they could hear him. "Are you kids alright?"

"Would ye like to fuck my sister?" the boy standing closest to the water asked.

"Excuse me?"

"She's only twelve. The men in Kenova really like her."

Teague was speechless.

"We had to leave Ashland. One of the men tried to short me and I stabbed him in the kidney. Got 'im from behind."

The boy reached into his trouser pocket and came out with a small dagger.

"Where are your parents?"

"You want her or not?" the other little boy said.

"I need to be going."

"No one said ye could leave." The one with the dagger took a step toward Teague.

"Is there somethin' wrong with her?" The other one pulled down his sister's dress. The tattered garment fell to her knees. The girl's underdeveloped breasts and battered ribcage made Teague heave. He hadn't eaten so nothing came out. He brought the dragoon from behind his back.

"Step back," he told the boy holding the dagger.

Although the boy showed no alarm at the sight of the gun, he did as he was told.

"Throw it into the river." Teague waved the dragoon toward the water.

The boy tossed the dagger into the water.

"You can pull your dress back on, sweetheart," Teague said to the girl.

The girl bent down and pulled the straps of her dress back over her shoulders.

"Now I'm going to get on my horse and ride away. If I hear footsteps behind me I'm going to turn and I'm going to start shooting. I'll just assume that whoever's behind means me harm."

Teague took another step backward toward the horse.

"Sir," the girl said.

"What?" Teague's voice broke.

"We ain't eaten hardly nothin' in three days."

"I'm sorry."

"We tried to kill some birds but my brothers can't hunt for shit. Willie's blind in one eye and Carl's kind of slow. No one'll help us and every time we try to sneak on someone's property we been caught. We'd be grateful for anything you could spare."

Teague kept the gun trained on the children as he undid his saddle bag. He pulled out Walter's gold watch and chain, the only thing his brother had left him. The farm had gone to his nieces and nephews, the slaves eventually set free.

"Did any of the places you tried to rob have horses?"

"Yessir," the girl said. "We weren't gonna eat no horse."

"I can't believe you, Lucy," the boy standing by the river said. "We could be full right now—"

"We ain't eatin' no horse!" she turned to her brother and screamed.

"Children!" Teague interrupted.

They stopped arguing and turned to him.

"Do you think you can get to the horse without being detected?"

"You bet. It's just up the bank past the trail. Man who owns it's an old fucker. He's always passed out drunk."

"You bring me back a horse and this is yours," Teague said. "I'm sure it'll keep you fed for a while."

Teague left the children jumping up and down in the silt, passing the gold watch and chain between them. He asked them if they had ever been to Mercy.

"We heard Mercy was kind of a rough town. A feller told us it wasn't no place for children, even ones like us."

At first Teague felt the urge to defend his city, to tell the kids that it had gotten better since the years immediately following the war. Then he remembered the night's events and the seeds of corruption planted by Thurman, Mills, and Walton. Pretty soon the town would be as bad as it had ever been, if not worse.

"Good advice," Teague said.

Teague told them to stay on the river trail where it was well lit and to get fed as soon as they could.

He would ride the nag they stole for him until it dropped dead and then remount Powder. He glanced back over his shoulder at the joy he'd propagated and a tear came to his eye.

He spurred the horse up the bank to the river trail, hoping to make up for some of the time he lost waiting on the riverbed. Strangely it felt like using the only thing Walter had left him to help those children was his amends for not saying something more loving to his younger brother before he left for the war and for not trying to contact him while he was gone.

He felt a calm come over him.

His gesture had not been entirely selfless. They had found him the horse, a decent wage for a job well done. But had they come back empty-handed, he believed he would have given them the watch and chain anyway.

If what he'd just done was not enough to keep Walter's ghost at bay, the journey he had undertaken would surely suffice. Perhaps if he survived, the dreams would stop.

He waited until he had gone around the bend and the children were out of sight to let the hammer down on the dragoon and place it back in the saddlebag.

27

The porch planks creaked outside.

"It's Ray Mallard," Scoggins said, peering out the window. "He's a foreman over at the iron factory. Bad drunk. I arrested him a few times for shooting at horses."

"Seems logical company for him to keep," Tompal muttered.

"He ain't been causing too much trouble lately," Hayes said.

"What do you call this?"

Hayes joined Barmore and Wanda, aiming his Spencer at the double doors.

"He's just standing there," Scoggins said.

"Hayes," a deep voice thundered from outside.

"What you want, Mallard? You got ten seconds then I'm firing through the door."

"I got a message from the reverend."

"He armed?" Hayes asked Scoggins.

"At least it don't appear so," Scoggins said.

"You may step inside, Mallard. Keep your hands where I can see them or you'll find out whether there's any truth to Thurman's horseshit about the hereafter a lot quicker than you might've been plannin'."

"Hey," Tompal whispered to Barmore. "We need some hammers and nails? You got any handy?"

Barmore nodded. "Downstairs. I do my own repairs. Don't like getting fucked by—"

"Grab you one of your whores and go downstairs and get every hammer, nail, and piece of loose wood you see."

Hayes let Mallard in, jabbing him into the middle of the foyer with the Winchester.

"Say your piece and be on your way," Hayes said to Mallard. "I'll extend that ten seconds to twenty."

"Thurman ain't after you or your deputy." Mallard's voice cracked at the sight of the barrel still aimed at him.

"I figured as much."

"He's simply adjudicatin'."

"He's what now?"

"I don't know what that means. I'm just relaying what he told me. He said he wasn't having no repeat of what happened with the Chiles murder. That we doing a right-eous thing here with or without you, Marshal. All we want is them two."

Mallard nodded to Tompal and the mute.

"Oh, is that all?" Tompal cocked both eyebrows.

"Anything else?" Hayes asked Mallard.

"I don't think so. I'm trying to remember if I left some-thing out."

"I think we get the picture." Tompal pushed Mallard through.

"Banks..."

It was all Hayes could get out before all hell broke loose. As Mallard stumbled onto the porch backward, Tompal shot him in the face for all the congregation to see. A chorus of gunfire sounded, glass on the far side of the foyer shattering, wood splintering from the banister.

All inhabitants hit the floor.

"Go gather all them items we just discussed," Tompal screamed at Barmore, who had sought refuge behind an upturned craps table with two of his whores.

More shots sailed through the foyer.

"Banks you just shot that man in cold blood," Hayes said.

"Kind of like you were doin' left and right in the middle of the main street. This is war, Marshal."

Something about Tompal Banks' demeanor rang familiar to Hayes, the way he carried himself in crisis. "I don't see you moving, whoremaster."

Tompal fit one of the revolvers into his belt and began checking the load on the other while Hayes searched for an argument.

"We have to secure these windows, Marshal, or we'll be dead within an hour. Especially once they find our weapons cache. There's a lot a guns in that wagon. About enough to arm every one of 'em out there. We're stuck until the cavalry arrives."

"At which point you're still going to jail."

"We'll burn that bridge when we cross it. That noose out yonder's a little more immediate."

Father Garrison handed the reins of his mare to Selma, who sat atop her mule staring down at him, forfeiting the fight she waged against her eyes, her pursed lips catching the tears as they trailed down her cheeks.

He knew no one from Holy Innocents was going to try

to stop the furthering of the bloodshed.

Hearing the shots from the bottom of the mountain, Garrison had ridden ahead, dismounted, and peeked from the corner of First and Central to see the two they had temporarily sheltered fending off dozens of armed townspeople; most of them Garrison recognized as converts to Thurman's mad Baptist ministry. Standing with the two outsiders was Marshal Hayes.

The father had no way of knowing if any of them were still alive. He and Selma had taken the long way to Holy Innocents, stopping by many a deacon's homestead. No doors were opened, no welcomes or assistance offered for those in need of genuine, selfless Christian charity.

"Go inside and wait in my quarters," Garrison said, refusing to look at the stone facade of the Church to which he had given so much of himself and from which he had drawn only derision and mockery. Even the thought of his parishioners did not bring him comfort, for where were they now?

He was glad he was wearing the red flannel shirt and jeans of an everyman. He felt it inappropriate to be dressed as a priest at this time, not just because he was done with their ineptitude but for the fact that he too was to blame. Instead of watching over the spiritual wellness of Mercy, he was assuaging his own base urges. "If you need to go down to the kitchen, if you're hungry or need anything go ahead. But don't go outside until I come for you or you get word that this nonsense is over."

"Please."

"The streets are deserted, Selma. Masterson's dead. Hayes and the two who came to us for help may be dead as well. If they're not then I am derelict in my neighborly duties by not assisting them in their plight."

"A neighborly duty? It isn't your duty to leave me behind to grieve for you. No one else is risking their lives."

"Well, despite all the work I've done here, the concept is still quite obviously foreign to these people."

The rest of the mayor's ride to Ashland proved to be much more difficult than he had counted on. Five miles after he'd left the children, the river road became impassable.

Heavy rains and six-team wagons loaded down with barrels of whiskey had left mud ruts that came almost to the horse's knees. After slogging along for almost three hours, he lost a good two hours riding across the swampy forest to the old road that connected Ashland to Lexington and Frankfort. What normally would have been a six-hour trip at an easy pace had become a nightmare.

The stolen horse died. Teague remounted Powder and stopped at the Russell Inn, a former stagecoach stop that still offered rooms, food, and drink to drummers and other passersby. He knew the large Russell family and their in-laws who often had come into Mercy to vote for him illegally in return for a cask of whiskey.

"Teague, you old sum bitch, you ain't runnin' again already, are you," roared Doc Russell, the lion of the family. "Seems like we just voted for you a few months ago."

"No, no, no, you did. I'm on my way to Ashland to fetch the militia," Teague explained, hurrying through the story. "Mercy's gone crazy and the mob is after blood."

"Well, you can't ride on an empty stomach. Berty, get the mayor a plate. Whatcha drinkin?"

"Whiskey, but I don't got time for food."

"By God, we'll go with you. Them sum bitches can't do that to Mercy. Hell, we wouldn't have any place to vote." Doc let out a roar of laughter, as did his four sons.

Every part of Teague wanted to reject the idea of allowing the Russells to join him. First, it would take them forever to get their guns, saddles, bedrolls, and whiskey together, and then they'd probably have to stop every mile or so. But, on the other hand, the Russells were a mean bunch that could defend him against road agents and other shadowy characters he might come across during his travels.

"Damn right," Teague said directly. "Let's get moving, men. Hell, we almost got enough to make up our own militia."

28

They nailed the corners of the roulette and craps tables to every windowsill downstairs, hammered plank boards over the batwing doors, and turned the second floor into a watchtower.

While the renovations were underway, Barmore introduced his whores to their new houseguests.

There were a total of seven girls who called The Brass Ass home. There was the star, Sydney, the seventeen-year-old pugilist of an Irish girl with a foul mouth and a dirtier mind. Gerty, the plump blonde who Barmore claimed could do things with her hands that would make you forget her rotting teeth. Christine, the oldest of the bunch, a fair-skinned lass who was missing an arm. Laila, a fitting name since her specialty was being able to spread her legs far and wide so men could experience depths they had never imagined. Sara, the mouthiest who filled the air with cock breath, advertising her prowess as if it were any other skilled trade. Chandra, the voluptuous former slave who Barmore exclaimed might be his favorite since she was as silent as the mute. And Wanda, whom everyone already knew.

The marshal asked Barmore if any of the other prostitutes were armed.

"Wanda broke the house rule." Barmore shot a disapproving glance at the fiery redhead hammering a nail through the roulette table into the sill of the north window.

"Would you rather me be at the mercy of these drunken bastards?" Wanda yelled.

Barmore turned back to the marshal. "I don't like my girls carrying guns or knives. It turns off the clientele."

"I ain't the only one," Wanda said.

"Bitch." Sydney dropped her hammer where she worked at the southern window and rushed over to Wanda. Barmore stepped between the women, grabbing Sydney by the wrists and pulling her arms behind her to stop the cat fight that was sure to take place if someone did not intervene.

"Sydney," Hayes said. "Wanda ain't rattin' anyone out. Right, Wanda?"

Hayes nodded for Wanda to agree with him.

"That's right."

"It's just that we need all the firepower we can get to keep them crazy bastards at bay. So listen up, girls. Anyone who's got any guns, knives, anything... I want you to bring it downstairs and lay it on the bar here. We just need to see what we're working with here, that's all."

The women stopped what they were doing and ran to their rooms on the second floor, returning moments later. When they moved away from the bar, there lay six revolvers, two sets of brass knuckles, and a throwing knife.

"I won't stand for this insolence," Barmore yelled.

"Things are lookin' up?" Hayes slid a .45 identical to his service pistol off of the bartop and maneuvered it into his empty holster.

"I don't know whose this is but I'm borrowin' it," Hayes yelled to the girls. "I hope ye don't mind."

He slapped Barmore on the back then walked over to help with boarding up the place.

Scoggins and Wanda stationed themselves in Wanda's room at the windows overlooking the veranda that faced Central Avenue and the cobblestone alley that ran between Tompkins General Store and the whorehouse.

Sydney and Gerty holed up in Sydney's room where there were two windows. One gazed out onto the bluegrass east of Mercy proper and the farms and houses beyond, the other onto the southern alley that separated The Brass Ass from The Tallulah Stables. Gerty armed herself with a .44 and Sydney convinced Hayes to let her have the Spencer, assuring the marshal in the plainest of language that she could fire the rifle as accurately as any man he would ever meet.

Hayes piled some of the leftover plank boards into the marble fireplace in the far corner of the gambling hall. He walked behind the bar, tipping his hat at the mute who kept lookout from a crack between the craps table and the sill of the southern window.

She made no gesture in return.

"Just bein' neighborly," he said, uncapping a bottle of bourbon and offering her a cheers before taking a large pull. "We are stuck with one another for the immediate future."

The mute resumed her vigil, studying the thoroughfare through the crack.

"I'll keep you company, Marshal," Laila said from the

bar where she sat next to the other whores who'd remained downstairs.

Laila finished the whiskey in her glass and twirled the dragoon in her left hand.

"I don't got no money on me, Laila."

"I'm bored. I'll throw you some on the house."

"I don't think that would please the man of the house none too much."

"He wouldn't have to know." Barmore had taken his sawed-off upstairs with him to join Scoggins and Wanda. "You could have me right here on the bar?"

Hayes shook his head no.

"What about you, outlaw?" Laila swung her stool toward Tompal, who sat with his legs propped up on the only craps table left in the gambling hall just in front of the northern window. "You want to come a little closer? Maybe have a little tussle?"

"I'm fine just as I am, thank you," Tompal said.

"It may be the last you get for a while, Banks," Hayes said. "You may want to take advantage of it. You'll either die here or get hanged within the year. Go on. I'll turn a blind eye to it. You ain't been that much trouble since I put you in your place up on the trail."

"I been thinking, Hayes, maybe when that state militia does arrive me and baby child'll be saying our goodbyes to you," said Tompal.

"I'd like to see that trick."

"You could just look the other way. She did save your life. And as you said if this is about you and me, you proved your point. You caught me. You beat the shit outta me. By the way I didn't exactly understand why you were so mad. I could have shot you dead and I didn't. You'd think a man might show some gratitude."

"I ain't got nothin' against you, Banks. Unfortunately, I am the marshal of Mercy and the two of you are wanted in Virginia and West Virginia for all kinds a charges, including murder," Hayes said. "And now in Mercy for questioning in the killing of Clyde Tanner. His wife—"

"Did you do any investigating into that murder?"

"Yes."

"Anything look out of sorts?"

Hayes didn't answer.

"That sounds about right."

"There's still the other charges."

"And after all we been through, Marshal."

"After all you done, Banks."

"I don't wanna hear it. You see, Marshal, you got yourself a little problem. You ain't gonna disarm us because you need all the help you can get, but you know good, and well, I'll shoot you and run the moment I take notion to do so."

"I could have fed you to that mob the second we rode into town."

"And you didn't. I'll give you that. Some would say it was your duty not to, you being law. But most, law or not, woulda handed us over to 'em gladly."

Footsteps sounded down the stairwell. Hayes and Tompal turned their attention to the bottom steps where Scoggins stood, waving as he stepped to the bar.

"Ain't you got a job to do?" Tompal said to the deputy.

"Wanda's got it covered," Scoggins said. "There ain't no activity down there right now. I need a drink. Hand me that bottle, Hayes."

Hayes handed it over without bothering to reprimand

the lawman in dereliction of his duties.

"You feel like telling us why you had all them guns now?" Scoggins asked.

"The blacksmith in West Virginia," Tompal said.

"The one you killed," Hayes said.

"He had himself a little side business," Tompal continued. "He was a retired Union soldier and must have been buying them cheap from some friend that was still in the service. We heard of him while we was in Virginia. He was drunk and running his mouth about all of the spoils he brought back with him from the war including a vast collection of guns. When we broke into the house to steal the guns, we found several models that had been issued in the last few years, many of 'em still in their oiled paper. So we figured it was only a collection for the purposes of sale. I know a man in Falls City that would have offered a pretty penny for those crates. Too bad the holy rollers got 'em. I guess the blacksmith wasn't the only one to suffer a loss."

"I figured it went something like that," Hayes said.

"Why'd you kill all them people?" Scoggins stood with the bottle, walking over to the table where Tompal sat.

"Deputy," Hayes admonished as he limped over to the fireplace.

"What? I'm just askin'?"

Hayes removed his coat, folded it and placed it on the oak floor. He lay down on his back, using the coat as a pillow, and placed his hat over his eyes.

Tompal did not bother to look up, to pay any heed to Scoggins other than to say lowly, "Seemed like a good idea at the time."

29

Erastus Mills shuffled into the empty saloon dragging his bad leg behind him and pulling himself forward with the help of his walking cane. He placed the cane on the bar and fell onto the stool beside Thurman, who stared ponderously across the bar at his reflection in the mirror above the rows of bottles.

Ike and the other members of the gang stood guard outside, reverently allowing the two their conference.

"No time t' lose composure, Rev," Erastus said.

"The circle is breaking. The center cannot hold, Erastus," Thurman said, proud of the quote. "We were going to hang the nigger to make a point and leave him dangling for the marshal and the mayor to see. Hell, I didn't even agree to killing the deputy."

Beads of sweat trickled down Thurman's face as he spoke.

"Well, we always wanted to show 'em that the Good Lord runs Mercy," Erastus said. "And ye wanted dem three strung up. Ye think any of this comes cheap?"

"Innocents have died."

"To make an omelet you gotta break a few eggs."

"Erastus. We have lowered ourselves. We're just as bad as the ones we're condemning."

"Enough with your bellyachin'."

"Erastus," Thurman said. "Do you understand what is happening? There are now innocent lives between us and the killers."

"You mean whores?"

"There's Hayes and Scoggins."

"Both drunken, whorin' bastards."

"It's my job to save them from eternal damnation, Erastus. Not send them there."

"Well, if they're aidin' them that you think the Devil sent, maybe they's beyond savin'?"

"I'm not sure anymore. How do I know who's beyond saving and who's not? All those people dying out there. I haven't seen anything like it since the war."

"Shook ye up?"

"Yes."

"Yer not so sure it's our duty to string dem up now?"

"I don't know. It's all so muddy. You know I have these episodes where my thoughts just seem to enter in one ear and leave out the other. How did it come to this?"

"We wanted to send de town a message. Dis will send de message loud 'n clear. There's more of us than dem."

"Doesn't it bother you the prospect of killing so many civilians?"

"No more den dem civilians escapin' to testify against us? Hayes got a clear look at me, you, and my son standin' on dem steps out dere. We got too much at stake with dis land deal."

"I don't think I can do it."

"I figured dat much. Just like you couldn't put together

dat land purchase. Just like you couldn't do nothin' without me, Reverend. That's why I'm takin' over this siege."

"What?"

"You're a goddamn puppet in dis operation. A face. And yer weak and getting weaker. Them sores are spreadin' and you ain't got what it takes to do what needs getting done. From here on out, ye say what I tell ye to say and ye preach yer little gospel to keep them sheep faithful to our plan."

"They are my people, Erastus, and I will tell them what words I hear from God." Thurman placed his palms on the bar, pushing himself up from the barstool. "And if I am unsure of something. I will testify so!"

Erastus gripped his cane and smote Thurman across the temple. Thurman fell back, toppling onto the sawdust floor with the barstool, landing on his side. He started to sit up. But Erastus dropped from his barstool to his knees and slapped the reverend with his bare hand, knocking him back down. Thurman cupped the lower half of his face in his hands as he wept. He removed them, examining his bloody palms.

"Deke and Roy'll keep ye company in here," Erastus said, leaning over him. "I'll tell yer ministry that ye ain't feeling too well. Wages of sin and whatnot."

"I've been honest with them about my past, that I'm paying for what I done when I rode with rebels."

"Then they'll be sympathetic. I'll tell 'em ye left me in charge of the siege."

"You can't do this, Erastus."

"Rev, we don't know how long we got till help comes for them. I'm guessin' a day or two at the most. We gotta infiltrate that cathouse 'fore then. With you runnin' things that ain't likely to happen. Don't worry none. As soon as it's over we'll talk. We'll come to some sort of understandin' you can live with."

"Did you ever even truly repent for what you did to that girl? Or was it for the land? So you could hide your money and continue on with your pillaging and your Godless ways?"

"Thurman, when I whupped up them tears for ye about that little halfwit whore after my baptism ye know why I was really cryin'? Because of how long it would take te build my kingdom through you so that I could have all the little whores I would want. That part of me still works, by the way. When we git our own fifty acres, our own school and farms and church, you know how easy it'll be. And I'll be an important man because, after all, who donated the bulk of the money?"

"You, Erastus," Thurman said through his tears.

"That's right. Pleasure doin' bidness with ye, Reverend."

30

The mute fell asleep in front of the smoking fireplace across from Hayes. Tompal had told her that it was all right, that he could see the entire street from where he sat.

Scoggins had finished half of the bottle at the bar and sat facing Tompal, who made every attempt not to encourage the slightly drunk and consequently inquisitive deputy.

"What are them markings on her face?" Scoggins motioned with his Winchester.

"Hell." Hayes pulled his hat from over his eyes where he lay on the other side of the dying embers. "I don't know how she sleeps through yer yackin'. Did she learn to turn her ears off too?"

"They're Apache scars," Tompal answered for her. "She was raised by them somewhere out West. They killed her ma and her sister. They took her and marked her to make her one of their own. They took her tongue to keep her silent on one of their treks through enemy territory. She was crying too much, apparently, and it was dark as pitch out, nothing but the desert and the painted faces of savages around her. Probably thought she had died and gone straight to hell. She was only four years old."

"How do you know all that, Banks?" Scoggins said.

"She has ways of communicatin'," Tompal snapped back at the deputy, the first time he had shown any emotion since the lawmen had known the killer. "You saw. Plus, I conjectured a bit. It's a rational explanation. Why would they adopt her and then do something like that to her?"

"How did you wind up with her?"

"I suppose she didn't exactly consider them family the way they done her. You know white men won't have nothing to do with a woman soiled by Indians. She ain't stupid. She may have been only seven but she'd heard talk. She knew the implications of what they done and that if she ever got rescued she'd be considered damaged goods. She hated them for it, but at the same time they had gotten in her blood as I'm sure you saw today while we was besieged by them lunatics. With no hope of living a decent woman's life, of becoming a gentleman's bride or even an asshole for that matter, she made her decision to return to the world anyway. She played house with the Apaches, gained freedom within the tribe, and escaped when I found her in Montana. That's about all the details I could get. She didn't really want to talk about it too much."

Tompal laughed at his own joke.

"What's her name?" Scoggins said.

"How am I supposed to know? She can't fuckin' talk, remember."

"Couldn't she write it down?"

"She can't write too good."

"What do you call her?"

"I don't call her nothin'. I either say 'hey' or 'get over here' or 'wake up' or 'you hungry'? She ain't so wrapped up in herself like a lot of these women nowadays. If I have to address her directly I call her 'girl' or sometimes 'baby child.' She seems to like that. It's a very pleasant setup we have."

"If she can communicate, how come you ain't never asked her name?" Hayes said. "She could have mouthed it to you like we saw her do earlier."

"It just never came up. I wouldn't expect you to understand us, Hayes."

"Why's that?"

Tompal grunted and turned his face away.

"Why wouldn't I understand?"

"We was a family the three of us."

"A family?" Hayes laughed.

"Yeah, Hayes. A family. You should understand that word, coming from such a Christian community and all. See, I read the Bible all the way through and it's written in there several places that we're all related. We're all brothers and sisters. So me calling them two my family ain't as far-fetched as that stupid look on your face makes it seem. I know it may not have looked like it, but we was. Families gotta show one another respect. Whatever her name was before them savages gotta hold of her don't mean a damn thing now. She'd just soon hear 'girl' or 'baby child' and if that's what she wants, it's fine by me. I don't expect you to understand, Marshal, because family is probably something you corn-fed types take for granted."

Hayes jumped to his feet and towered over the outlaw, his trembling index finger a half inch from Tompals' face.

"You ever talk about my family again, Banks, and I'll make you beg for the mercy of that noose outside."

"I apologize," Tompal said after a spell. "I don't know

nothin' about you or your people. Family's a sacred thing, ain't it, Marshal? At least we agree on something."

Hayes returned to his side of the fireplace.

"Can she even make sounds?" Scoggins said.

"Yes. I've heard her on a few occasions when she was in some pain or somethin' tickled her. But she don't prefer to. I think she's a bit sensitive about it."

"What about you?" Scoggins said.

"What about me? You repeatin' yourself, Deputy? You askin' me why I killed so many folks? I thought we been over this."

"I just wanted to know how ye turned out the way you did. Most folks ain't wanted in three states."

"I grew up in Knoxville. My mother was a whore. My father was her master. I killed him one night with his own .22 rifle after he had tied her to a bedpost and whipped her with a belt until she bled so bad she passed out. I was watching through the crack in her door from the hallway. Went into his room—they had a room they shared and a guest room where she turned tricks to pay for his opium and his gamblin'—and I grabbed his gun and walked back in there where he stood over her cursing and calling her names like he liked to. I shot him twice in the back of the head and carried my mother to town. The only man for miles who knew anything about medicine was a retired doctor who had been one of my mother's most frequent clients. When I knocked on the door his wife came out and ordered me off of their property, told me my whore of a mother could bleed to death for all she cared, said she guessed her man wouldn't be stepping out no more. She shut the door on us. My mother died in my arms that night in an open field not a mile from that house."

"And somehow that explains why you killed all them people?" Hayes said.

"After the first it's easy."

"That's a hard hand ye got dealt there, Banks" Scoggins said.

"I'm going to shoot one of you if silence does not descend upon us shortly," Hayes said. "I for one need at least a few hours shut-eye before daybreak."

Before Hayes replaced his hat over his eyes, he noticed the mute awake, soberly eyeing Tompal in the firelight.

31

On the porch awaiting, Erastus, Ike, Deke and Roy stood facing The Cap' n' Ball's doors forming a semicircle around Father Garrison, who was oddly dressed in a flannel shirt and jeans, his hands raised in a surrender gesture.

Ike took in the bloody street beyond his lieutenants and then the priest before speaking.

Morning had broken over Central, shades of gray and blue providing the thoroughfare a backdrop that did not betray the barbarism of the night preceding nor that which the flock's regency had planned.

"We told him he could put his arms down," Ike said.

"Put yer fuckin' arms down, Father," Erastus said. "Before ye render 'em useless."

Garrison slowly drew his arms to his sides.

"What can we do fer ye?"

"I came to speak with the reverend," Garrison said. "I thought this is where I might find him since your son Ike and these other three men were standing guard out here."

"I'm impressed," Erastus said. "Walkin' up here like this took some grit, Garrison. Was ye scared?"

"Yes."

"Any of the congregants give ye trouble on yer way over here? I didn't hear no shots?"

"No."

"Just dirty looks, I suppose? Well, they're a bit on edge, what with them Devil's spawn holin' up in our Christian community. I'm sure ye understand."

"It's no problem. Really. I would just like a word with Thurman, one man of God to another. If it isn't too much trouble that is."

"Trouble is," Erastus said. "Rev ain't feelin' too well. Maybe ye could tell me what's on yer mind and I could get him the message."

"I think it may be best I speak with him in person."

"Like I told ye, Father, he ain't feelin' too well. You know he's got health problems. Hell, Thurman couldn't hide his condition if he wanted to with that shit all over his face."

"If Thurman's fallen ill then who is in charge here?"

"I'm in charge."

A horrified look fell upon the priest's face.

"You can't be serious."

"I'm serious as an undertaker. Now, ye better turn around and go back the way ye came."

"Erastus, you have to stop all of this. People are dying."

Erastus cocked his good eye at his son standing behind Garrison.

Ike hit Garrison in the kidney with the stock of his Winchester. As the priest collapsed to his knees, Erastus raised his cane and brought it down upon Garrison's shoulders.

"You two." Erastus waved his bloody cane at Roy and Deke. "Drag this good Samaritan in there with his fellow shepherd and keep an eye on them until we've flushed our quarry out of that cathouse."

Roy grabbed the fallen priest by his legs and Deke took his arms. When they lifted him, straining the deep gashes on his shoulders, his scream reverberated throughout the streets of Mercy.

Hayes awoke to a cacophony of screams. He sat up to see Barmore and Scoggins holding onto Tompal's arms as he writhed and thrashed, pulling the two men with him toward the boarded doors, the mute standing by the bar, hesitantly taking two steps forward and then one back, not sure what approach to take.

"I'll kill 'em," he yelled. "You can keep my bullets to defend yerselves. I'll kill 'em with my bare fuckin' hands."

The mute finally stepped between Tompal and the door and placed a hand to his face. She caressed his cheek, complementing the rotations of his eyes so that he could not look away from her.

"The priest," he lowered his voice. "That priest that took us in, baby child. They beat him right there on the street."

She shook her head, indicating that she understood.

"Which priest's he talkin' 'bout?" Hayes peeked out the crack between the roulette table and the windowsill. The street was empty of activity. Leaning on the porch rails of the saloon, Ike and Erastus Mills stared back.

"Father Garrison walked over to The Cap n' Ball, I guess to have a word with Thurman," Scoggins said. "He exchanged some words with the Mills gang and they wound up doing quite a number on him. Ike hit him in the kidney with his rifle."

The men allowed Tompal to drop to his knees, feeling him give up the struggle. "The one who drew the sword on us that was walkin' with the cane."

"Erastus Mills," Hayes said. "He used to be a road agent until that preacher reformed him and his gang. At least that's the rumor."

"He don't look too reformed to me. He hit that man while he was down. Hit him across the shoulders with his cane. Then they carried him in that saloon, pulling on him where he'd been hurt."

Hayes was at a loss. This cold-blooded killer was having a complete breakdown because of the beating he had been forced to witness.

"Why do you care what happens to Garrison?" Hayes joined the others gathering around Tompal, the mute now kneeling beside him with her head on his shoulder, caressing one of his hands.

"Before you caught us, that man took us in and fed us like we was one of his own," Tompal said. "Like we was family."

It hit the marshal like a snowfall in June.

Hayes choked up, averting his gaze as he stood, picking a corner of the room to lock eyes upon.

"Yeah," Hayes said.

"Father Garrison was the one that did your marriage, wasn't he, Don?" Scoggins said.

"He's a good man," Hayes said. "I never trusted a man that smiled more than I do and them priests over at Holy Innocents are a bunch of smilin' sons of bitches. All of 'em 'cept Garrison. I always liked him. The few times I'd give confession I'd make sure he was in to take it."

"What concerns me is what part Erastus Mills has to play in all of this," Barmore said.

"Me too," Hayes said.

"That fellow makes me look like a clergyman."

"And he ordered Garrison to be flogged without Thurman present," Scoggins said.

"Makes you wonder who's running this carnival," Tompal said as the mute helped him to his feet.

PART FOUR

The Banks of the Ohio

32

It took all morning to explain to his lieutenants the plan's intricacies, to gather the wayward flock, and to arm them with the contents of Tompal's wagon. It would take that much longer to explain it to the congregants who would play vital roles in the siege.

It was now afternoon and luckily the elapsed time had not taken any of the bloodlust off of the faces of Thurman's ministry.

Erastus hocked a wad of phlegm onto the planks under the hanging man's slowly swinging feet, the rafter above creaking as the rope swung from side to side. He nodded to Ike, a gesture that communicated a paragraph, a talent they had developed during their time as highwaymen. The congregants were all present, now armed with the spoils the killers had been hauling. Ten had remained in the alleys behind and across from The Brass Ass, watching for any activity or escape attempts.

"As ye all know," Erastus' voice cracked as he attempted to project it. "My health ain't what it once was, so my son Ike will speak for me. I have instructed him on the situation."

Ike stepped forward on the other side of the hanged man.

"The reverend has fallen ill," Ike said. "You all know of his condition and it wouldn't be fittin' for me to speak of it. But he's left it to my daddy to run the show until he's feelin' better. He's upstairs in the sleeping quarters having himself a rest. Until then, will the following people please come forward? Erastus has duties to disperse."

Erastus cupped a hand to his mouth and leaned in to whisper to his son.

"Milton Skinner," Ike yelled.

Skinner stepped forward without the crude disguise he usually wore during Thurman's services, his face now in plain sight.

"Will Chiles."

Will ascended the porch steps. He laid down the double-barreled shotgun he had wielded during the battle.

"I'm done," he said.

"What?" Erastus snapped.

"I don't want no part of this no more."

"You want to see another father go through what you did?" Ike said.

"No. That's why I'm calling it a day."

The crowd parted as he turned his back on the congregation.

"Fuck him," Erastus whispered. He then dictated the next name to his son.

"Abe Tremont," Ike yelled.

Ike called out the names of ten more men. Besides Skinner, those who stepped forward were all Confederate veterans.

Erastus allowed Ike and Roy to begin debriefing the

others in the stables where those in the cat house could not overhear. He then sent Skinner on his chore, to ride out to the Mills house to retrieve the one crate from their arsenal they had neglected to bring back to town in the wagon earlier when they thought this would all be over in a matter of hours.

The two men who addressed one another as Mr. McMahon and Mr. Sleadd observed the proceedings in front of the saloon from their carriage on the northern end of Central Avenue.

The street was thick with blood, filled with mutilated and bullet-ridden corpses of both sexes, the fading embers of decumbent torches revealing the eternal thunderstruck expressions of what the dead had witnessed in their final moments.

Jutting out of an alley to the right of Mercy's new guests, a wagon tied to two eviscerated mules was splayed out on its side. Opened crates lay in the street next to it, shells of assorted calibers spilling out.

"There goes our gesture of good faith," McMahon said, turning his horse around. Sleadd followed without question, as was his duty. "Let's see if there perhaps exists a local with a capacity for reason or logic that might tell us something."

They retraced their path onto First Street that had fed them into Mercy from the mountains west. They stopped at Lexington Avenue, immediately west of Central, taking notice of a sign pointing south, advertising the direction of the courthouse and the city jail.

* * *

McMahon righted one of the chairs and took a rest in the middle of the jail. He lazily uncapped the bottle he had noticed underneath one of the drawers that had fallen out of an upturned desk.

"Take your coat off," he said to Sleadd, who still stared through the bars at the dead deputy. "Stay a while."

McMahon raised the bottle to his lieutenant and took a long pull.

Sleadd crossed his arms and leaned against the bars, waiting for McMahon to further direct him.

"I've never seen anything like this," McMahon said. "There's been some sort of coup. You know what that means?"

Sleadd nodded that he did.

"They killed this deputy, a few of them dying themselves in the process and now they've gathered in front of that saloon, somehow having obtained our weapons, to rain further havoc upon this community. How many wagons hauling crates filled with enough rifles and ammunition to, well, I guess take over a small town? How many of those do you think could be traveling through this state in one day? You're a man of few words and that's a rhetorical question anyway. In all probability, not that many. Perhaps one. Plus, there's the Negro, like the one Peterson described we saw hanging from the saloon rafters. So, Tompal shows up with his guns and his gang of rogues, perhaps commits a crime or maybe not. It could be word of his exploits simply arrived here before we did. Anyhow, the inbred locals then lose all sense of decorum and due process and revert back to their most basic states. The rest is history as they say."

McMahon took another drink.

"I suppose going after Tompal Banks at this point wouldn't be very cost-effective. There's a lot of those sons of bitches out there and there's no point competing with them for the privilege. I'm just worried they'll fail, Sleadd. They're ignorant and I have a feeling this man's not, even though he has made a lot of mistakes and left a lot of bodies in his wake. But he hasn't been caught yet, and everyone who has tried has wound up a lot worse for wear. I don't have any faith in someone else executing our revenge on this man."

McMahon motioned grandiosely to the wreckage of the jail and the body in the cell.

"It's just hard to stand this kind of a loss, Sleadd. We lost the guns, the cash we put down, and the income we could have been raking in while riding around in the mountains like a couple of perfect fools trying to speak the language of these backward hill people. I mean to tell you I am fucking angry, Sleadd."

Sleadd stepped from the corner shadows into the light of the open doorway, his hands in the pockets of his overcoat. He stared beyond his seated overlord, breathing meditatively.

"This prick cost us," McMahon said lowly. "And not only do I not get my revenge, I can't even have faith that those with the means and the desire to kill him will pull it off, because they lack the simplest of resources men like us take for granted, such as opposable thumbs and self-consciousness. Tompal Banks came like a carpetbagger and absconded with what was rightfully ours. What kind of country do we live in where a man can do that and get away with it?"

33

"If you're gonna die, might as well go out with some style?" Scoggins spoke from behind the bar where he was mixing himself a Mint Julep.

He toasted the black beauty across from him and tested the foreign mix of fluids. "Hmmm. That's a helluva a drink, Chandra. Why did I not try one before death was knocking at the door of a whorehouse I found myself trapped inside?"

"Why did I waste my life spreading my legs for meager wages?" Chandra said. "I should go cut that shitheel Barmore's shriveled balls off right now before one of them holy rollers gets the chance."

"Come on now, Chandra. I'll pour you a Julep."

"I don't know what worries me more," Hayes said, "the different disasters that could erupt in here or what they're up to outside."

He watched the congregation disperse, marching from The Cap n' Ball's plank boards to the empty stables.

Laila was drinking gin straight from the bottle, disgruntled that no one was paying her any mind. The mute was still asleep in front of the cold fireplace.

"That's quite a deputy you found yourself," Tompal said.

"You take what you can get."

"How was the other one? The one you lost."

"You being smart?"

"No."

"He was a good kid. Hell, he wasn't a kid no more. But nonetheless he was good at his job. We served in the war together and he helped me through it when we came home."

"You know I ain't a bad man."

"I suppose all them people just stepped in the path of your bullets while you was shooting at bottles."

"It's complicated. It ain't all one way or the other."

"Ain't it?"

"You get put on a path, Hayes, and it's hard get off it. You said you fought in the war, right?"

"That's what I said."

"And then what? You ran for marshal?"

"Sort of."

"Watcha mean 'sort of'?"

"Some people thought I'd be good for the job and they kind of did all the work for me."

"Some people who knew you'd run things their way."

Hayes thought of Councilman Walton and his stomach turned.

"What's your point?"

"My point is, what if they hadn't? What if you came back with no legs and no one wanted nothing from you? You'd still have to get by somehow. You got a position in the community, Hayes. You're able to eat. It ain't that simple for some folks."

"Tompal, when I look at you I don't see any missing limbs."

"What about her? You see anything missing there. You think anyone anywhere is going to take her into their community?"

"They ain't gonna stone her."

"Not exactly."

"What's that mean?"

"That means there're predators out there. Folks that love it when they find someone who's different, someone who's been cast aside. They look for any sign that separates you from the flock and in turn makes you weaker 'cause you ain't got the protection of a community. And when you got one as apparent as hers, you're always a target. They don't have to stone her, Hayes. They just leave her out for the wolves."

"And you protect her."

"The results of which usually involve encounters with holier than thou types such as yourself."

"I don't hold myself above anybody."

"Just people hard on their luck, I suppose."

"You want I should feel sorry for you, Tompal? Maybe spread a donation plate around."

"I don't want nobody feeling sorry for me. But I want it understood that everything I done I had a reason for doing, being as I might not survive the next sunrise. I never roamed the countryside plundering and pillaging aimlessly. Anyone I killed either tried to harm her or tried to jail us. Also, there were far less of the latter in my further defense. And you know that woman was the one shot her husband just like baby child said. Well, she didn't say it. But you understand what I mean."

"Why do you care what I think?"

"You might live."

"And what then? Most people are still gonna think of you the same way?"

"Okay, I lied. It ain't about you livin'."

"What's it about then?"

"I thought we might've been friends if things had been different."

"Shit."

"I ain't kiddin', Marshal. The first time I saw Cody I knew we was gonna be friends. Same thing with the mute. It's kinda the way I felt the first time I laid eyes on your haggard ass, Marshal. 'Cept, unfortunately, you was fixin' to arrest me, so I don't think the friendship had a fair chance to ferment."

"You just looked at me and thought, me and that fella would hit it off great?"

"And everything I've learned about you has confirmed the fact."

"Like what? Me and you ain't nothin' alike."

"Sure we are."

"Name one way."

"Right off the top of my head."

"If there's so many, Tompal, that shouldn't be too hard."

"We both know what it's like to see our loved ones taken from us."

Hayes grunted and limped toward the bar.

"That we do," he said, ignoring the outlaw and talking to him at the same time.

"Change your mind, Marshal?" Laila asked drunkenly as Hayes passed her.

"I'm going to get some more shut-eye."

"Maybe you'll stick yer cock in the freak over there instead." Laila motioned to the mute with her glass.

Hayes ignored the inebriated whore's jibes as he wadded up pages of the *Kentucky Gazette*, a stack of which sat on the stone mantle for burning next to a box of matches. The marshal looked down at the mute who lay awake on her side then back at Laila, hating her for what she'd said.

"Don't listen to her," Hayes whispered. "You ain't a freak."

The mute shifted her vision from the empty fireplace to Hayes, who knelt to revive the flames.

"I'm serious. Don't listen to her or anyone else that thinks they know somethin'. When you get to be my age, it's kind of nice to see a pretty woman that looks a little different."

The mute sat up, a grin widening in the light of the match Hayes had struck on the stone mantle.

"We all got scars, darlin'," Hayes said.

34

Surprisingly to Teague, the rest of the ride seemed to go much faster as the more the men drank the more vulgar their stories about each other and the louder their laughter grew. Their longest stop was at a place called Flatwoods, which consisted of a string of houses and a store a few miles outside of Ashland.

The men soon found the local watering hole, and took full advantage of it for both themselves and their horses. There, too, men at the bar wanted to join the excursion, even though they were not sure of its purpose. Teague decided enough was enough and thanked the drunken men for volunteering their service. The Russells were also too sloshed to ride. Teague left them in their cups, conversing loudly in a drunken language only they could understand.

Powder gave out just outside of Ashland and Teague wept over his dead horse as he headed on foot to William Culbertson's house, figuring it would be better to have the mayor with him when he asked the militia for help.

Culbertson was a jowly, red-faced fellow who smiled more than any man Teague had ever met and was not at all perturbed that the Mercy mayor had woken him, throwing on his robe and offering Hayes his daughter Sara's mare to accompany him to the barracks.

The headquarters of the Kentucky Militia were in a dilapidated Civil War-era hospital that had barrack facilities for about sixty men, although there were only twenty-five in this squadron.

The men were not soldiers, but were something of a ragtag unit of lawmen. Each had a badge, a .30-30 Winchester and a Colt peacemaker. Each trooper was a crack shot, drunk or sober, which made anything else they did, on duty or off, just fine with Teague.

"There's stretches when they find themselves with a lot of time on their hands," Culbertson explained as they waited for the door to open. "They're prone to getting into a little trouble themselves."

Culbertson held an invisible bottle to his open mouth.

"I see," Teague said.

The sleepy-eyed militiaman who opened the door was of indeterminate age. He had short, thinning gray hair and a face like ancient leather but the build of a man half his age.

Culbertson introduced him as Captain Charles Sellers.

Teague held out his hand for Sellers to shake and the captain just looked at it, turning and leaving the door open for the two to follow. When Teague entered the vast barracks with Culbertson, the other militiamen were waking from their soiled cots. The room was bereft of any other furniture except for a collapsed desk in the corner and a year-old calendar on the wall.

Teague explained to the captain the crisis in Mercy, and when he was done, Sellers guffawed, refusing to converse any further until Culbertson pulled rank and vouched for the mayor of Mercy's sanity. The problem then became convincing the men to mount up. Sellers' concern was over the number of river towns for which the 17th Brigade was responsible.

"That's the problem with these river towns," Sellers grunted. "They're full of river rats. Mayor, there is no end to the worry towns like Mercy bring to my brigade."

"The steamboat trade does bring an element—"

"You know how many instances like the one you just described we've had to deal with in the past few years," Sellers interrupted. "Too many to count. There didn't used to be a brigade in Ashland until 1877. They got tired of having to wait to send for the one in Frankfort. With all the people we have on these banks displaced by the war and the type that work the steamboats, the governor knows towns like Mercy need us nearby."

"And we're thankful."

"The problem is, every time I answer the call and stifle these uprisings, you mayors always send letters to the governor complaining. Apparently my way of doing things don't sit too well with you political types."

"What way would that be?" Teague asked.

Sellers removed a glove and slapped it against his palm, causing Teague to flinch and take a step back.

"The only way to deal with a pack of rabid animals."

Teague was a little hesitant at this point but realized this man was his only hope and continued to grovel for Sellers' help, promising no complaints would come from the mayor's office or the city council.

To the vexation of many of his lower ranks, Sellers finally agreed.

Twenty-six men rode out of Ashland, including the

mayor of Mercy, armed and ready to rescue what survivors might await them in the river township ahead.

The mayor rode on a stud furnished by the state.

Outside town the brigade halted at the sight of the steamer's crew stepping onto the wharf, just off the river road, thick black and gray smoke rising from the stacks, the paddle wheel still in the shallow waters where it docked at the end of the short pier. In cursive lettering across the side of wheelhouse read The River Rat.

A young officer named Maddox, one of the better mannered of the men, had whispered to Teague not to agitate the captain for the man was mercurial, prone to unpredictable mood swings that could last any length from minutes to weeks, leaving as quickly as they came.

Teague asked how such a man gained and, more to the point, kept a commanding position in the state militia.

Maddox told him that Sellers had something on a certain statesmen and was loved all throughout the city of Ashland for his heroics in the Civil War. And besides, Maddox told the mayor, the captain's oddities were roundly overlooked as it was universally accepted that any sanity he lacked had been sacrificed nobly for the South.

"Do you know how fast a steamboat can travel downriver?" Captain Sellers asked Teague as he drew his .45.

"What are you doing?" Teague panicked.

"We can make it to Mercy three times as fast if we take that boat."

Sellers fired in the air and the men walking toward the shore from the boat halted and faced the mounted brigade.

"I'm Captain Sellers of the Kentucky State Militia," he shouted. "What happened here?"

"Suicide." An oafish man in a pea coat and a five-point

captain's hat spoke as the men behind him parted ways, revealing the corpse that they had just let descend to the boards. He was a handsome blond man that looked to be no older than twenty-one, his eyes closed. There was no blood on him anywhere, and had Teague not been told, he could have easily believed the young man was closing his eyes to protect them from the afternoon sun.

"Suicide?"

"Yeah."

"Jesus," Teague whispered.

"Drank a full bottle of laudanum," the steamboat pilot said. "Must have bought it in Cincinnati. Found it empty in his quarters. Guess he didn't like the river life no more. Plus there's cause to believe he might have had the syph."

"What kind of freight are you hauling?"

"Steel. Just dropped it off in Cincinnati."

"How far is that man's home?"

"He's from Ashland."

"Well, I hate to interrupt your ceremony, but I'm going to need you to take whoever's necessary to run the ship and get back on board because we're in dire need of transportation."

"This man needs to be taken to an undertaker."

"So take him," Sellers said. "Send a few of your men into town. Ain't there enough that you don't need that can carry him?"

"Well, I suppose—"

"Okay then. We're going to board your ship now. Can that thing carry horses?"

* * *

At first Captain Charles Sellers thought the girl lying on the river trail was a victim of road agents such as the henchmen of the syphilitic reverend described by Teague. Sellers ordered the pilot to stop the paddle.

The captain called for Teague and Officer Maple, a stout man with a patch over his left eye, to join him. Considering how close they were to Mercy, he thought the mayor might recognize the girl. They guided their horses to the shore and rode up the bank to get a closer look at the body.

The fringes of her dress were ripped and bloodstained, her right eye puffy and blackened.

Maple remained horseback while Sellers and Teague dismounted. The captain drew his Winchester from its sheath as he approached, pivoting with each step, rotating the gun's aim from one tree line to the other.

"I gotcha covered, boss," Maple said, winking at Teague with his good eye. "Anyone peeks out them trees gonna feel a taste of rock, salt, and nails, I can tell y'all that much," Maple cackled as he tapped the stock of the shotgun lying across his lap.

Teague was careful not to stare at the eye patch. The man already looked silly displaying a permanent sneer with the cigar sticking out from between his teeth. His ridiculous laugh always ended in coughing.

"She's alive," Sellers said, removing his index finger from her neck.

"I know her," Teague said. "That's Lacey Newmyer."

Teague had to catch his breath at the sight of the bottoms of her blistered, bleeding feet, results of her ten-mile walk. Whatever she had seen in Mercy had not made her any fonder of the town, judging from the lengths she had gone to escape it.

"What do you make of this, Mayor?"

Maple would never call a man by his Christian name. Sellers was Boss. Teague was Mayor and the rest of them were shit.

"She was actually with Thurman's congregation when last I saw."

"What do you think that means?" Sellers examined the bloody knot on the back of Lacey's head.

"It can't be good," Teague said.

"I think it means more hell's broke loose in Mercy since you been gone," Maple said.

As the wide Ohio River rushed on beside them, they discussed the odds, specifically the unlikelihood of their own survival, and the even lesser chances that the lawmen were still alive.

"Forty?" Maple said.

"Probably more," Teague said.

Teague lay against the cabin deck with Lacey's legs across his lap, her hands clasped together, her arms locked around his neck to keep her upright beside him. Her blood-matted hair fell across his shoulders.

"That's double what we got. Shit."

"What a waste," one of the younger men riding behind Maple muttered.

Sellers turned in his saddle.

"Who said that?" he said, staring right at the sweaty, hawkish young man who had spoken. "Speak up, Warner."

"If they's already as good as dead," Warner said, "why're we goin' to all this trouble? I'm goin' get myself killed on the off chance two lawmen and a coupla no-count tramps might still be alive."

"There are civilians to think about also, Warner," Sellers said.

"The mayor's been sayin' they was targeting a gang of killers. That just don't seem to be a cause worth dyin' for, Captain. Man'd have to be a fool to think otherwise, you ask me."

"No one asked ye," Maple said.

"You can go home if you like, Warner," Sellers said.

The eyes of every man were trained on the officer in question.

"I'll have the pilot stop and you can get off."

"All right then."

Warner's grin faded as Sellers cleared his revolver of its holster.

The officer had brought his hands out in front of him but was soon halted in his gesture and blown clean off his horse, blood rising from the crater the bullet dislodged from the left corner of his temple.

He fell to the hull, his body shaking in lifeless spasms for a moment until Sellers shot him again, removing the other side of his forehead, at which point the young militia man's body went limp.

"The Kentucky State Militia does not tolerate deserters," Sellers' voice boomed throughout the valley. "Is that understood?"

Maple descended from his horse and kicked Warner's body into the water that crashed against the hull.

Sellers had his answer.

35

"Here." McMahon handed Sleadd the bottle he had drained dry on the ride from the Mercy jail. "I am not afraid to admit it. You have a better arm than me."

Sleadd heaved the empty into the river where it made a light splash, then a series of ripples, sinking and then rising back to the surface seconds later where it floated, drifting slowly down river a dozen or so yards from the shore where they stood.

"I'm drunk, Sleadd." McMahon drew his piece. "I thought for some inane reason that achieving this state might calm my murderous urges."

McMahon fired at the bottle, a splash appearing near its neck, pushing it farther downriver faster.

"But I was wrong."

He took another shot and missed again, hitting closer to the bottom, the wave knocking the bottle back in the direction from which it had started.

"Look at that." McMahon lowered his gun. "This Banks situation's got me so riled I can't even shoot straight. The South and its people are contagious. They are infecting this once-reasonable Ohioan with their generations of handed-down depression and ignorance. Herbert Spencer would have taken the idea of survival of the fittest a step further had he made his way below the Mason-Dixon Line in his lifetime. He would have rewritten it 'removal of the weakest' because they always bring us down to their level, Sleadd. Always. The whores I peddle and the gamblers whose debts I sometimes have to collect in flesh, I pray a safe return to their familiar pleas and excuses, as pathetic as they are, for those aggravations are but minimal compared to the unacceptable insults to human dignity that I have witnessed on this journey. At least Cleveland's lower class can speak proper English."

He fired twice more, missing by several feet this time, the bullets penetrating the water far from the bottle that now floated downriver.

"You care to have a go?" McMahon said.

Sleadd pulled back his coat flaps at his hips and crossed his arms over his chest, whipping both dragoons from their holsters. He fired off two shots in quick succession, shattering the bottle's neck and then its bottom, the guns vanishing back beneath his coat.

"I might be perturbed if you were not in my employ," McMahon said, pressing down the ejector rod with his index finger as he rolled the revolver's cylinder with his thumb, discarding hot shells onto the silt at his feet. "Let's put behind us this wretched land and try our best never again to speak of it."

McMahon stared at the silt and mud beneath him for a moment, trying to shake the aching feeling that he had been duped out of time and money by such arbitrary forces, this meek land and a man he had never laid eyes on.

When he brought his chin up, Sleadd was pointing south

just beyond the wharf at a slight bend in the river. Above the mountaintops rose a cylindrical cloud of gray-black smoke.

When the steamboat appeared from around the bend, McMahon sat beguiled by the sight of the armed and rugged horsemen on the hull.

The paddle slowed as the boat approached the banks where Sleadd and McMahon stood at the end of the side road that led west to Mercy proper, halting at the wharf. Some of the men unsheathed their Winchesters, injecting rounds at the sight of the two strangers.

From the shadows beneath the cabin deck stepped an older gentlemen with a face made of soaked rawhide and an expression to match. In his right hand he clutched a Colt beside his head, aimed at the sky.

"Drop your weapon," the old man barked. "Identify yourselves."

"I should request of you the same courtesy, sir," McMahon shouted back across the riverbed, fitting into his revolver's chamber another fresh round.

"I am Captain Charles Sellers with the Kentucky State Militia. We have come to restore peace to the town of Mercy and to escort to safety those whose lives are in jeopardy."

"Well, Captain, if you were going to restore peace, why then would you need to escort anyone to safety? Are you not confident in your mission?"

"I will ask you once more to identify yourself. Then you will be shot down for I will be forced to assume you are part of the riotous mob that has caused our presence here today."

Sellers cocked his revolver, leveling it at McMahon and

Sleadd while his men followed suit.

"That won't be necessary, Captain." McMahon holstered his gun. "I am Herbert Spencer and this is my esteemed colleague Henry Sidgwick. I own an extremely successful hotel in Chicago as well as a few bars and restaurants. I am growing tired of the city life and was taking a tour of the South to find some farmland to purchase and someday settle on to live out the rest of my days in peace."

"Let us come ashore and we'll talk further," Sellers said. "Keep your weapons holstered or you'll be shot dead. There will still be armed men aboard this boat while some of us forge the river to the banks. Am I understood?"

"Yes, sir."

"Sellers," Teague said as the captain mounted his horse. "I need to accompany you."

"That is preposterous. I can get us to the town from here. We simply follow that road up the bank west to Mercy. You are a civilian and I am not going to allow you to endanger your life. You ain't the only one waiting on the boat. I need men here to return fire from the water in case we're followed back."

"Don't you need me to guide you through the town?"

"I think I can manage. The road where most of the damage took place is Central Avenue, correct?"

"Yes, but..."

"It runs north and south. Lexington, the road where the jail is located, where the deputy was killed, runs parallel to it. How many roads going north and south could there be in the business district of Mercy?"

"Dammit, Sellers."

"What is it, Teague?"

"I'd be wary of those men on the bank. I think they're

lying about their names."

"Do you recognize them as part of this Thurman's congregation?"

"No."

"And they talk like Yankees."

"But Herbert Spencer is a..."

"I'm not taking you with us, Teague," Sellers said to the mayor. "I know it's your town and you have an interest you wish to watch over. But my main concern right now is getting those prisoners, the lawmen, and any other civilians who need help, out safely. If I can accomplish that, I think the fires of unrest will die down on their own since the mob will no longer have an enemy to target."

"I certainly hope none of these men are educated," McMahon whispered to Sleadd. "Herbert Spencer? That was a risk I would not normally take. Oh well. Chalk it up to inebriation I suppose."

Sellers was the first to make it off the wharf and onto the silt.

"We saw what happened in Mercy." The captain's grip was firm and oily, the Yankee utilizing all that was left of his intestinal fortitude not to wince or heave.

"Perhaps you can paint me a picture," Sellers said. "We only have one eyewitness account and she was bedridden when she gave it."

McMahon described the dozen or so mutilated bodies that now littered Central Avenue and the crippled man whispering to the younger one as they stood on the porch next to the swinging Negro, the younger one then rattling off names to the crowd gathered before them, members of which would immediately come forward as they were called.

"Then we fled," McMahon said. "We rode so fast my horse knocked loose a satchel carrying some of my most prized belongings. It's back there now amidst those lunatics. It was surreal to say the least. We assumed we were bearing witness to the aftermath of some sort of slightly botched mob justice."

"There are four people in particular we believe to be the target of this mob." Sellers said. "The town marshal and deputy who are protecting a pair of wanted killers, a man by the name of Tompal Banks and his female companion, a mute. Banks is in his early to mid-forties, has black hair with flecks of gray. The mute has these tattoos on her face, blue lines running from below her eyes down to her jaw. No one seems to know her name. You didn't happen to see anyone who fit those descriptions?"

"I can't say that I did. Sidgwick?"

Sleadd shook his head.

"However," McMahon said. "There's an establishment called The Brass Ass. I assume it's a brothel. All the downstairs windows were boarded up and I could see faces peering out the ones on the second story. There were several dead people on the porch. In the alleyways across from the brothel as well as beside it, stood men and women with guns and farm implements. You might want to start there."

The other militiamen were now ashore in formation awaiting their orders. McMahon took count; there were sixteen of them including the captain.

"Could you use a hand?" McMahon asked.

"You're civilians," Sellers said. "I'm afraid I can't put you in harm's way."

"That is not entirely true," McMahon said. "Both Mr.

Sidgwick and I are volunteer firemen."

"And that don't make you civilians?"

"They don't call for civilians when a fire breaks out in my neighborhood, Captain Sellers. They call for me. My point is that you are going up against a town of armed madmen. There must be fifty of the bastards. How many of you are there? I count sixteen. The odds are not in your favor. It seems to me you should take all the help you can get. And it also seems that our positions as volunteer firemen create a nice loophole in your 'no civilians' rule."

"Actually, he's got himself a point there, Captain," Maple said.

"Do you have any identification validating any of this?"

"It's in the satchel I lost fleeing Mercy."

The captain examined McMahon from ankle to eye as if the northerner was on the auction block and Sellers was a bidder.

"You've run into burning buildings and quenched raging fires?"

"Yes, sir." McMahon grinned.

"What kind of experience do you have with weapons?"

"Sidgwick here is the best shot I have ever seen." McMahon patted Sleadd on the shoulder. Then tapping his revolver said, "I'm not too bad myself either. We've had to defend the hotel against thieves and drunkards on many an occasion. Would you like us to prove our prowess?"

"That won't be necessary. I think we can use y'all. Just stay in formation with the men and follow my command. You think you can handle that?"

"It will be refreshing to have the burden of running the show removed, Captain. Lead the way."

36

"Thad," Wanda shouted from her lookout spot at the veranda window facing Central. She was pointing at something across the street, bracing herself against the wall by the sill when Barmore came in from across the hall where he had been checking on Sydney and Gerty. At least that is what he said he was doing. Wanda figured he had probably taken Sydney into his quarters to get a piece of her little Irish delight.

"What is it?" Barmore reeked strongly of female loins and had that elated, ruddy-faced expression men get when they have just sowed their oats.

"There's movement on the second floor of the boarding house," Wanda said.

"I don't see anything."

"Not anymore. But just a moment ago two figures appeared in front of both of them windows, vanishing just as quick."

Barmore rubbed lust's aftermath from his eyes and stepped out from behind her to take a closer look, squinting as he bent with his hands on his thighs.

"Wanda, I don't see a—"

"Don't stand directly in front of there like that, Thad."

Wanda slapped him on the shoulder with the back of her hand as the projectile burst through Schultze's second floor and soared through the pane from which the pimp was staring. Barmore placed his palm over his eye and staggered a step back then stood to face Wanda, who was now backpedaling away from the open range of the pane.

The flesh peddler let his palm drop and Wanda screamed, the room behind Barmore fully discernible through the hole where his eye had been moments ago.

More cracks sounded, tiny holes appearing in the windowpane, shots imbedding themselves in the mattress behind her, tearing to pieces the painting above the headboard that depicted Mary Magdalene as a brothel whore wearing garters and a corset, a halo above her head.

Sydney and Gerty rushed into the room, both ducking as a shot shattered the unlit lantern on the table beside the bed.

"They're shootin' from the boarding house," Wanda screamed with her hands over her ears. "The second floor."

Gerty rolled across the bed and edged along the wall to the window facing the stables. Sydney dropped to her stomach and crawled around Barmore's corpse to the side of the veranda window opposite, breaking out the bottom pane with the Spencer's stock. She glanced back over her shoulder at the dead pimp as she turned the gun barrel toward the boarding house. Her eyes glistened with tears.

She faced the broken pane and began firing at the windows across the thoroughfare.

"Wanda," Gerty said, alarmed at something she spied out the southern window. "I need you over here, honey."

From the thatched roof of the stables below, two men

dressed in tattered suit coats and trousers stained heavily dark red were making their way toward The Brass Ass, both with torches in their hands.

"Why, that's Delbert Wells." Wanda pointed with her gun. "He works at the stables. He used to be a regular of mine. And that's Abe Tremont. Barmore had to ban him from The Brass Ass. It was before your time. He got drunk and chased me around my room with a Bowie knife. Wanted to carve his name into my hide. I had to pull this damn Webley on him. Came this close to shootin' the bastard."

Abe and Delbert reached into the inner pockets of their suit coats, coming out with two red cylindrical objects. They held them up to their torches, sparks igniting at the ends of the cylinders.

The men were holding sticks of dynamite.

Abe pulled back his arm to catapult the stick toward the whorehouse.

"Well, shoot him now, Wanda," Gerty shouted, raising her dragoon.

The women blasted out the windowpane, Tremont dancing below them as the shots tore through his midsection and he dropped the explosive, falling beside it, its wick igniting the others creeping out of his coat pocket.

Sydney pulled the trigger on the first shooter, watching the figure descend out of sight, in the dark of the room beyond the window pane.

"One down." She turned to her friends, hoping for them to share in her victory.

But they were preoccupied.

Gerty and Wanda were watching Delbert panic on the roof below. He placed his own unlit explosive at his feet and began pulling the sticks out of Tremont's pocket and rolling them down the other side of the roof. He hit the deck just as the blast shook the foundations of the neighboring buildings, a red fireball mixed with a thick cloud of black smoke immediately following.

Downstairs, shots pierced the tables the besieged had nailed over the windows. Smoky, dust-filled sunrays lightened the darkened gambling hall.

Tompal backed out of his chair and edged along the wall toward the southern window while the women at the bar, along with Scoggins, who had been mixing his third minted cocktail, dropped to their stomachs.

"It's coming from the upstairs of the boarding house," Hayes shouted across the hall to Tompal, peeking through a small space beside the craps table's edge.

The mute stumbled, half awake, from the fireplace toward the windows, shots piercing the leather of the bar beside her.

"Get down, baby child!" Tompal screamed.

She pivoted left and braced herself against the southern wall, inching along until her coat sleeve was touching Tompal's.

"Scoggins," Hayes bellowed. "If you ain't gonna use that Winchester, you mind tossin' it over here? I ain't gonna be able to hit shit with this pistol."

"I'm gonna go ahead and try," Tompal stood back and placed the barrel through the space between the edge of the roulette table and the sill. "I can't hardly see the window to my right, Hayes. You'll have to take that one. I'm shooting north."

"Got it," Hayes said. "Scoggins."

Scoggins' forehead appeared from behind the bar just as a shot perforated the leather inches from his skull. He quickly reclaimed his hiding place.

Tompal took his first shot as the mute crawled under the window, positioning herself across from her partner.

"Scoggins!" Hayes yelled.

Scoggins shot up, tossing the Winchester to Hayes and dropped back behind the bar without a word.

Hayes was swinging the lever and opening his mouth to thank his deputy, sarcasm in his throat as the words formed, when the first blast came, knocking him off of his feet, the Winchester sliding across the floor beside the mute who had been brought to her knees.

Tompal remained poised by the windowsill, firing with distinct discipline as the floor below him and the ceiling above shook from the explosion that was not far off.

"We only have a half crate of dynamite," Ike Mills said, standing next to Erastus as they looked out onto the state of warfare they had engineered. "If we don't get one in there your plan goes to hell."

"Don't wurry," Erastus said. "It'll get in there."

"Abe lasted a matter of seconds. I still think it would have been better to light all twelve sticks and leave them in the back alley."

"The idea, ye fuckwit, is to take out as many of them while sacrificin' as few of ours and wastin' as little time as possible. If we take out the second floor, the ceiling will implode on top of those downstairs. Two birds. One stone. Simple really. Of course I forgit that a halfwit bag o' horseshit like yerself can't comprehend even such elementary concepts."

"When this fails, I am going to laugh in your face," Ike said. "When they shoot Delbert like they shot Abe and we ain't got no one left—"

"Ye of little faith. You think them's the only ones I got crawlin' around on rooftops?"

"But you said when you told us your plan—"

"I told you what you needed to know."

"Who else is up there?"

"Turns out Milton Skinner has quite the throwin' arm. Claims he can toss horseshoes like ye wouldn't believe. He told me when I asked 'im to fetch de dynamite he could help in other ways. I think all dat killing yesterday might have sprung something loose in 'im. Had dat bloodlust in his eyes. Ye know how it is yer first time. I say he's willin te werk. Let 'im. I warned 'im though that a stick of dynamite ain't as heavy so he should make the proper adjustments."

"That's very pious of him."

"All's well that ends well."

"Like I said. I'll be laughing in your tired, crippled face before this ends."

"De day you laugh at me I really will believe some God made you rather than my couplin' with a broke-down whore."

Ike reached for his pistol but stopped short of the holster. His hand wavered in the air beside the butt of the gun, trembling.

"I hate you," he whispered, turning his back on his father and brushing past the saloon doors where the holy men lay captive.

* * *

"Get up, Marshal." Tompal peered down at Hayes. "They've stopped shooting from the boarding house but we got another problem."

Chandra and Laila had taken up arms, on their knees firing from under the nailed up craps table where Hayes' post had been.

A louder gunshot than those coming from the upstairs boarding house windows blew apart three of the plank boards that barricaded the front door. Hayes pushed himself to his knees and looked out a hole the size of a saucepan that had been blown out of the middle of the swinging doors.

The congregants swarmed upon Central from either end of the street and from the alleyways across, armed with the same farm tools as earlier, as well as the vast array of weaponry from Tompal's wagon.

Hayes dropped down on all fours, crawling under the northern window on his knees and elbows, holding the Winchester to his chest like the guerilla soldier he had been in another life, creeping up on wandering Union squads while they slept or conversed carelessly by firelight.

He stood erect on the far side of the window, levering a round into the Winchester's chamber.

The face of the first man he got in his sights was obscured by the muzzle flashes of the two .44 revolvers flailing in his hands.

Hayes took him down and Geraldine Tanner took his place, the barrel of a Sharps buffalo rifle resting on her shoulder, eyes fixed on the ministry's target, void of any empathy for those inside. She appeared as some sort of demon that had risen from the earth, the whites of her eyes aglow, her only human features turned stoic behind the dirt and dried blood that caked her face.

Hayes had her in his gun sights, a round in the chamber ready to fire but he could not bring himself to shoot down the troubled woman whose lies had started this snowball to hell.

Tanner swung the rifle in an arch across her breasts, catching its stock as she dropped down to one knee. She looked Hayes in the eye, then squinted as she aimed at the crack in his barricade.

Gerty and Wanda had both lost their footing and fell onto the mattress as Sydney was knocked against the brass bed frame, the Spencer spilling across the floor in front of the doorway.

"Sydney." Gerty reached through the rails of the bedpost and turned her head to see red droplets trickling from a deep gash in the girl's hairline, her eyes closed. Gerty shook her by the shoulder but Sydney did not move.

Wanda sat up from the bed and stared back out the southern window. Her eyes bulged and she dropped to her knees scanning the floor for her Webley.

"Gerty!" Wanda yelled.

"Wanda," Gerty cried. "Sydney won't wake up!"

More shots shattered the veranda window, one tearing through Sydney's forehead, covering Gerty in brain matter.

Gerty rose to her knees, screaming as she stared at the bits of scalp thick with black Irish hair that had landed in her palms.

Wanda lifted the quilt and looked under the bed, her eyes spotting the Webley. She reached and grabbed it, rising to her knees as the dynamite landed at her feet. She licked her thumb and snuffed out the wick.

Down the hall where they had abandoned their post came the sound of glass breaking. Wanda crawled across the mattress, dropped to her feet and sprinted down the hallway to Sydney's room. On the floor amidst the debris of the window facing the eastern fields lay a bundle of dynamite sticks tied together, their wicks entwined and burning. She placed her heel on the sparks and breathed deeply as she removed her shoe, finding the explosive dismantled.

Feint and staggering, she made her way back down the hallway to find Gerty fumbling as she lifted another stick from the mattress, its fuse all but burnt out as she extended her arm to toss it back at Delbert.

The wick hissed, the ball of fire that resulted consuming first her arm, then Gerty and Sydney behind her and then the rest of the room in one awful explosion.

37

While the women upstairs struggled to diffuse the dyna-mite, Hayes had resigned himself to shooting this pathetic creature, a female to boot, squeezing the trigger slowly when Tanner lowered the rifle, standing and turning her head in the direction of the arcade and the boarding house. Like dominoes in reverse, the rest of the congregants rose in a wave of alarm at the unmistakable, overbearing sound of a herd of horses galloping toward the town, growing nearer with each hoofbeat.

Tompal and the women to his left lowered their weap-ons, ceasing fire in reverence for the sounds that signaled possible deliverance.

The horsemen rode out of the alley howling like rabid pack animals, their faces set in permanent battle cries as they fired upon the congregants from above. All of them were dressed in fatigues of light brown and flat brim hats, boots pulled over their pant legs except the two ghostly pale men in the back who wore black overcoats and Stet-sons, slaying each man and woman they took aim upon.

"Let's do 'em the courtesy of meetin' 'em halfway," Tompal said.

"You just stay where I can see you." Hayes began pulling down what spindly wood was left boarded to the front door. The mute and the whores joined in, speeding up the process.

"What happened?" Scoggins stood shamefaced behind the bar now that they were no longer under fire.

Hayes didn't bother to answer, stepping back for the women to exit first.

The mute stopped short of the doorway, standing there between her partner and the marshal.

He waved his hand, motioning for her to go ahead.

"I have to go upstairs and make sure Barmore and the other girls know," Hayes said.

"Ain't you worried about us runnin'?"

"I'm more worried about the people who sheltered us."

"Are we saved?" Scoggins asked.

The second blast came seconds before the roof imploded. Instantly, a beam of wood swung down and crushed Scoggin's skull as one of the whore's brass beds dropped down onto the bar, the dead deputy disappearing underneath as the rest of the ceiling fell.

Maple swung his empty shotgun stock-first, knocking free the front teeth of one of the crazed mob members running toward his horse. He spurred on to the porch of The Brass Ass, dropping the gun in the mud and drawing his revolver, firing into the mass of sneering faces closing in on their formation.

He turned to check on Haskins who had been riding beside him, a newer recruit who spoke with a stutter.

The dead youth was being dragged by his horse, his left

foot stuck in the stirrup. Another militiaman fell in front of him, Maple's face showered in scarlet as the private was blown from his saddle.

When they made it to the porch planks of the cat house, there were ten left.

The front doors of The Brass Ass cracked open and the men who had traveled all day to ride into certain death were greeted by five well-endowed women toting pistols, their faces made up to match the loud, elaborate gowns they wore.

Sellers held out his hand and pulled up the Negro girl, resting her on his lap.

Without having to be told, the surviving militiamen rushed to the others, crowding the women between the horses.

"Return fire, you fools," Sellers screamed.

While the lucky few lifted the women horseback, the rest joined McMahon and Sleadd, who continued to hold back the depleted mob. McMahon had grabbed a rifle from the hands of a woman he had brained with his revolver and was making good use of it while Sleadd continued hitting every mark he sighted with his dueling dragoons.

As Maple helped the blonde woman up and she wrapped her arms around his gut, straddling him from behind, the earth shook, his horse bucking as the militiamen and the mob were showered in glass and splinters, the second floor of the whorehouse lighting up in a fiery roar.

The blonde hugged Maple's stomach so hard he felt he was going to pass out, but the smell of her hair cascading down his shoulder kept him awake.

When the fallout ended and the smoke cleared, Maddox and Bowman, another rookie, lay at the porch steps.

Maddox had been impaled through the top of the skull by a foot-long splinter of wood and a shard of glass slightly longer jutted out from Bowman's neck.

Their thoroughbreds remained unscathed, yards away from The Brass Ass.

Maple surmised that the steeds must have thrown the two men free when they bucked, leaving them helpless under a sharp rain of fire.

The mob had suffered less since they were farther back from the building, although Maple could spot a few fresh holes in the mass of bodies. It had diverted them from their purpose for a moment, many of them now on their knees and stomachs, in fetal positions to avoid projectiles entering any orifices.

"Any other survivors inside?" Sellers asked the Negro woman. His horse turned west, ready to lead the survivors back to the banks.

"Just us."

It was not the whore who answered, but the deeper voice coming from the captain's back.

He turned to the wreckage of The Brass Ass.

The three stood shoulder to shoulder at the bottom of the wooden steps, their faces blackened by soot, their hair littered with flakes of wood and glass.

The one with the mustache had a marshal's badge pinned to the breast of his ripped and bloody shirt.

The other two fit the descriptions of Tompal Banks and his female partner with the Indian tattoos.

Sellers pointed to the two riderless thoroughbreds.

"Mount up," Sellers ordered. "We're through here."

****

The priest and the reverend sat across from one another at a table in the middle of the saloon. Each man hid his eyes in the pits of his elbow, resting on the dirty table littered with sawdust trying to keep from passing out. The guards wanted them in eyeshot and would not allow them to rest on the floor. The reverend had fallen out of his chair twice, suffering several kicks to the stomach for his infraction.

Garrison placed his chin on his forearm, dragging it left and then right to see if the guards were looking.

Deke was leaning back in a chair, his hand clasped behind his head and his feet resting on a table facing the window, his back to the captives. Roy also stood with his back to the holy men, pouring himself a drink at the bar.

He whispered to Thurman, "Reverend."

The shots and explosions outside dominated all sounds in the room.

Garrison tried raising his voice and leaned in: "Reverend, we've got to do something."

Thurman did not look up.

"I've failed my flock, Garrison. I'm nothing but a hypocrite. I led them astray from anything resembling the Gospel. I'm going to burn for this."

"You're sick, Thurman. You were trying to do a good thing and it turned into something else. But we can turn this around."

"How?"

"They still believe in you. The Mills' are speaking in your behalf. They're lying to your people. If you get up and go out there and call this off, they're not going to shoot you. If they did that the mob would be on them like a bad case of syphilis—sorry—well, you know what I'm getting at. You have the power, Thurman. You started this and you can damn well put a stop to it."

The doors brushed open. Ike Mills swaggered in, taking the bottle from Deke's hands as he was lifting it to pour another shot. Ike took a swig, breathing hard out of his nostrils as he stared at the prisoners.

He stepped to the table, holding the bottle by the neck as he leered at Thurman.

"How'd it feel?" Ike said.

Thurman still did not look up from his arm.

"Look at me when I'm talking to you."

Thurman stretched his arm, laying his cheek on his shoulder, pleading with his eyes for the tormentor standing at the table's edge to leave him be.

"What is it, Ike?" Thurman said.

"How'd it feel?"

"How did what feel?"

"Having your thumb on me like I was some sort of errand boy for the holy order of horseshit you was preaching about? Dunking me down in that water and speaking of my life like it meant nothing until I met you, having all your crazies cheer at the notion?"

Thurman lifted his head, sitting upright with the help of his forearms, his swollen lips barely able to contain his smile.

"It felt great."

"What?"

"I love pulling lost souls from the reaches of hell. But I never liked you, Ike. I love you because you are a child of God. But if I had any say in it I would have dunked you in the river a second time and held you down quite a bit longer."

Ike tucked his coat flap behind the handle of his gun as

he took another pull off his bottle.

Thurman pushed himself up from the table, laughing in the face of the Mills boy.

"And I confess in the presence of this pagan priest that I indulged in the pleasure of hearing them laugh at you like the half-dead afterbirth they saw you for on the banks of the Ohio that morning."

Ike lowered the bottle to his chest.

"You want to hear a guilty pleasure I indulged in?" Ike said, examining the shallow amber liquid he had left to drink. "That little Chiles cunt you lost your mind over, the one whose murder they hung that vagrant for. I cut her head off before I was done with her because she couldn't take what I had to give. Little bitch was kind of ungrateful if ye ask me."

"You're right-handed?" Thurman's smile vanished.

Ike transferred the bottle to his right hand, tipped the neck in Thurman's direction, offering a toast.

"Who's laughing now?"

Ike had the mouth of the bottle to his lips and drained the last of its contents.

Thurman grabbed the chair behind him and flung it across the table. It sailed over Ike's head, one of its legs shattering the upturned bottle, breaking the mirror and the shelves of liquor across the bar.

Ike appeared to be choking himself but when he removed his hand from his neck, the priest saw that he had pulled free a shard of glass from the bottle, a crimson waterfall staining his white suit shirt, ruining his Sunday best. Ike fell to his knees beside Garrison, making gurgling sounds as he attempted to breathe. The priest grabbed the revolver from Ike's holster, training it on the two guards just now coming alert, their pistols still holstered.

"Give me that." Thurman snapped his fingers. "You're far too meek for such a task."

Garrison shrugged and tossed Thurman the revolver.

Thurman cocked it and shot the two men, aiming high and catching each in the forehead.

"Jesus, Thurman," Garrison said, watching Deke and Roy flop on their backs, the horrid smell of feces filling the barroom as their bowels evacuated. "Where did you learn to move like that?"

"I wasn't always a man of God, Garrison. I rode with Morgan where I learned to kill as efficiently as I learned to preach. Also, would you please not take the Lord's name in vain, Father. At least not in my presence."

"I'm sorry."

"It's okay. We are all guilty of sin. Now it's time for Erastus Mills to pay for his."

"Git after dem!" Erastus screamed, standing at the open doors of Tallulah stables. As if back on the battlefield, he waved his saber like it was a flag, hoping to ignite the mob that was low on morale. "Take a horse, each and every one of ye that can still use yer hands and feet. Git horseback and ride out, now!"

A break formed in the crowd that had been severely decimated by the militia's raid. A full half of them laid down their arms, turning their backs on Erastus. Those hurt headed east to seek medical attention from Doctor Hamilton while others simply gave up their faith in the fight and went home.

Geraldine Tanner had asked one of her fellow deserters

where the local undertaker lived. She was now headed to Christoper Newmyer's home with no money on her nor a way to transport her dead husband back to West Virginia. Perhaps this Newmyer fellow would have mercy on the newly widowed Tanner and assist her in making the proper arrangements.

She would not know until she got there.

Miles Skinner stared up at the gutted second floor of the whorehouse, imagining what the bodies of the people he killed must look like. He turned away and lost himself in the mass heading north on Central, away from Erastus's battle cries. He pried a revolver free from the grip of a dead pig iron worker and disappeared into the alley between the boarding house and the arcade. He checked the load, cocked the pistol, and stuck the barrel in his mouth.

"Have mercy on my soul, Father," he said, the barrel muffling his last words.

The shot only interrupted Erastus for a moment.

"Te hell wit' dem," Erastus said to the twenty or so men dragging themselves to the stables. They had picked up bits of burning wood from the rubble of The Brass Ass as they approached to use as torches as the night was now falling. These were the ones Thurman had the hardest time reforming, the opium addicts and war vets, some of whose exploits even impressed Erastus.

It made sense they would be the ones who saw it through.

"Can all of ye ride?"

His question was met by a round of decisive nods.

"Well, what the hell ye standing there for? There's more than enough horses here to carry ye river rat sons of bitches. Move!"

* * *

Erastus was calming down, standing upright with his cane dug in the mud and the blood below, watching the congregants disappear into the western alleys.

He breathed in through his nose and out through his parted lips, considerate of his condition and aware of how absurd it would be to die of natural causes at a time like this.

Two shots sounded in quick succession from somewhere behind him. He shifted his cane to turn back toward The Cap n' Ball.

Reverend Thurman was walking down the saloon steps, a revolver at his side and a grin across his bloody lips.

"Where's Ike?" Erastus said.

"He shouldn't drink so much, Erastus." Thurman spat blood into the mud.

"He got a little better when he started going te church."

"He was just holding back so I wouldn't suspect your deception."

"Where's my son?"

"I killed him. And he's in hell because he was lying when he said he accepted Christ as his Lord and Savior. And to be quite honest, the thought of it fills my heart with joy."

Erastus dropped his cane, raising his sword, and waddled toward Thurman, who allowed the saber to pierce his heart before placing the gun to the cripple's head and blowing his brains all over the walls of Tallulah stables.

38

The sun was long gone behind the foggy mountains on West Virginia's side of the Ohio River by the time the horses in front began to descend into the moonlit waters, toward the steamboat awaiting. The others stayed in two rows as they slowly made it down the bank to the wharf.

The mute clung to Tompal from behind. They rode next to Hayes near the back, the two men dressed in black overcoats just behind them with their rifles at the ready. Sellers had ordered them to help keep an eye on Tompal and the mute.

"So you're the infamous Tompal Banks?" The one without the scar nudged his horse beside the outlaw.

"Infamous is stretchin' it a bit," Tompal said. "Why ain't you dressed like the others?"

"Because I am not a soldier." McMahon lowered his voice as he slid forward the dragoon he had borrowed from Sleadd. "I'm a volunteer."

"You talk like a Yankee."

"I am a Yankee."

"What brings you down this way?"

"Business."

"What kind of business?"

"I was going to purchase some firearms from a man named Nathan Eble. I believe you know him."

McMahon stuck the barrel of the dragoon against Tompal's stomach. The impact of the blast threw him against the Mercy marshal. Hayes tried to hold onto his reins and keep the wounded outlaw upright but lost control of the spooked thoroughbred. Hayes fell with Tompal in his arms as the horse brayed and ran, causing the formation to do the same, stampeding faster down the slope toward the boat.

The two militiamen in the back were bringing up their rifles when the man with the scar pulled another dragoon from his coat. He shifted in his saddle and fired twice, turning back toward Hayes and the prisoners as the men dropped from their horses behind him.

The mute pounced on the man who had shot Tompal, knocking him clear off his saddle. He dropped the dragoon and they rolled down the bank as she beat his face with the butt of the empty Schofield.

"Watch out." Tompal pointed beyond Hayes who was rising to his knees.

Hayes spun around, dropping on his back and firing just as the man with scar got off a shot.

The man fell from his horse. Hayes shot him again where he landed a few feet up the bank.

Hayes tried to turn over to check his own wound but he winced, lying down and resting his head on Tompal's hip.

He looked down, touching his left ribcage from where the blood was flowing.

"They got you too?"

"Yeah. They got me."

"I'm sorry."

'What the hell you sorry for?"

"If I'd never shown up you'd still be alive."

"I am still alive."

"Where they get you?"

"I think it pierced my ribcage."

"Ye ain't alive if it nicked a lung."

"Appreciate the optimism."

"Baby child," Tompal yelled, staring down the bank.

When they landed in the silt at the water's edge, she dropped the bloody Schofield and began punching him with her bare hands until his arms and legs stopped moving.

She felt his wrist and detected a beat.

His coat lay open and she saw the Bowie knife in a sheath under his gun belt. She drew it and pulled at a hunk of his thick black hair, placing the blade to his scalp.

He was still alive when she removed it.

"I didn't tell ye all of it," Tompal said.

"All of what?" Hayes tried to lift his head but it hurt too much so he just breathed in, saving it for the final run down the bank.

"About me and her. I didn't tell ye all of it and I didn't tell ye the truth."

"I ain't a priest."

"Just listen. Please. I need you to know. You saved her. Look. She made it."

"We could still make it."

"I got it together for a while. It was a woman who done

it. You believe that? A woman tamed me. Her name was Rachel Bartlett and I met her in Louisville. That's right. I lived in this state for some time. She had red hair and the biggest brown eyes I ever seen. She robbed me with 'em, Marshal, the way I robbed men from Knoxville to St. Louis. She gave me her hand in marriage and I took over the livery her father owned when the TB took him. You know Louisville fell to the Union. I stayed out of it, didn't even think about setting off to war with the second chance I'd been given. I wasn't goin' to die for that bullshit with the life I'd been given. Then one day I came home from the livery to find my wife being held down by two Union soldiers, another spreadin' her legs and pulling down her undergarments. I broke one's neck and then the others restrained me, told me now I got to watch. And I would have too, had a troop of rebel soldiers not been passing by our property and heard her screams. They saved my wife. So I gave my life to their cause. Me and the rebels buried the Union men in our yard and I sold the livery to the bank, sent Rachel out West with my unborn child in her belly and her cousin, Roscoe, who had worked for me as an escort. I told her I'd come for her when the war ended, that I owed these men. We were lucky to get out before anyone came sniffin' after them dead soldiers."

"You fought for the Confederacy?"

"The 10th Kentucky. Gave 'em four years of my life to repay my debt to 'em. When the war ended I rode to Texas and after a year of searching discovered that Rachel and Roscoe had been killed in an Apache raid outside of San Antonio where they were living. I spent the next year tracking them Tonto Apaches, making sure it was the right ones. I slaughtered them where they slept, all of them but the white girl with the blue markings on her face they'd taken as their own."

"She's your daughter."

"Yes."

"Does she know?"

"No."

"Why not? Why haven't you told her, Banks?"

"Could you? Look at what they done to her? Look at what they done to her because I sent her out into them badlands without a father to keep watch over her. Because I went off to that goddamn war."

"We gotta go, Banks." Hayes sat up.

"Hayes."

"What?"

"Her name...her name is Jonna Margaret Banks."

"Okay."

"Promise me somethin'."

"What? We ain't got much time. The last of the horses is getting on. I don't know how long they'll wait."

"They can hang me, Hayes. I don't care. I'll confess to everything I done. I'll even confess to killing that Tanner fellow even though it ain't true. Just tell them that she was my hostage."

"They ain't gonna believe that."

"If you tell 'em that woman, the only other witness, was one of them crazies, then your testimony's the only one that'll count. It's you and the whores. Yours'll mean the most. Just tell 'em that from what you observed, you believed her to be my hostage and that it was all my doin', all the horrors perpetrated. She's got a chance to turn it around here. Especially if I ain't around."

"Were there any witnesses in West Virginia?"

"Shit. I guess I lost too much blood. I ain't even thought of that."

"I'll do what I can." Hayes slung Tompal's arm over his shoulder.

They staggered down the bank, moving as fast as their wounds and the slope would allow.

"You could marry her."

"What?"

"If you married her, Hayes, it would be different. You're a respected Confederate veteran within your community. Plus, you could tell the mayor and the city council to call in some favors on her behalf, couldn't you? I mean, the city kind of owes you since they left you to rot."

"You've lost too much blood."

"If you married her they might be more lenient. Say that you saved her from my clutches. It could work. What else are you goin' to do? Go back to rollin' drunks and pretending not to be one your own self?"

"I got nothin' to hide, Tompal. I am a good friend of John Barleycorn's."

"Do this for me," Tompal said. "She's sharp as a knife. And she's tough. And you know she ain't gonna mouth off all the time and give ye a lot of grief. She won't be no trouble, Hayes. She's basically self-sufficient. But she still needs someone to watch over her. They'll eat her up 'cause she's different."

"I can't believe what I'm hearin'."

"I think she's taken a liking to ye too."

"I don't think me marrying her would stop them. Especially if there's witnesses."

"Ain't it worth a try? Think of it this way. If it fails they'll hang her and you ain't any worse off than you was before."

Hayes gazed down the bank where she stood next to the one who had shot her father, her knees on his arms as she pulled loose his scalp. She then slit his throat and stood, throwing the scalp into the water and turned to see the men approaching.

Her tattooed face was flooded with tears.

"She's beautiful too."

"Yes, she is."

They had reached the silt when the torchlights illuminated the bank. Hayes glanced over his shoulder where the dirt road began and saw the line of horses, the congregants atop.

"I'll tell them what I observed when I examined the Tanner crime scene. That y'all weren't guilty of that."

"Well, I—"

"I'll map it out for 'em if I have to. Then I'll lie and say she was your hostage. I'll say when I caught you to bring you back to town she was already trying to escape you, that she led us to where you was hidin'. Scoggins is dead and he's the only one who can say otherwise. If there's enough varying accounts, they might not hang her, especially considering all that's transpired."

"What about the other thing?"

"And I'll do that too."

"Why you doing this for me, Marshal?"

Hayes didn't get to answer.

The silt erupted as the rifles and shotguns discharged from atop the bank. The boat was quickly heading north. The pilot had panicked when he'd heard the first shot. Sellers and the other surviving militiamen had made it on board with the whores and were returning fire from the hull.

The three standing on the riverbed had but one route to avoid the crossfire. Without speaking they discarded their heavy coats and boots and jumped into the freezing Ohio, bullets whizzing into the water as they immersed their heads and began paddling.

<h1 style="text-align:center">39</h1>

Teague reached down from the boat's hull and pulled Hayes aboard, allowing him to lie down on his back.

The gunfire had died down, the men at the rails aiming determinately east.

"Mayor Teague," Hayes whispered. "I am officially tendering my resignation as marshal."

"I understand."

"How hard did you punch Walton?"

Teague laughed heartily, joyous of his old friend's survival.

"Barmore said you knocked him on his ass."

"I take it Barmore didn't make it."

"No."

"He was a better man than I gave him credit for."

"A lot of them are."

"I'm going to go find you and the girl some blankets."

"We need to put pressure on this." Hayes motioned to his wound. "Bring me a rag or a piece of feed sack... something I can get dirty."

Teague stood and sprinted down the hull to the stairs that led to the cabin deck.

Hayes scanned the hull.

The whores were huddled together against the fuselage of the cargo area in the dark under the deck, holding hands and caressing one another back to sanity, allowing themselves the privilege to weep. Hayes recognized Lacey Newmyer's face among the women. He didn't bother to figure how she'd wound up on the ship. It didn't matter. She was free of her no-account husband and the brunt of his fury, at least for the time being.

Jonna Margaret Banks leaned against the rails. She shivered in the dark as she stared at the shore, drenched from head to toe. Her hair was matted to her brow and her shirt and jeans clung tightly to her curves.

Hayes rolled over on his stomach and gripped the steel rails, pulling himself to his knees as he searched the river's edge.

Tompal, clutching his bloody shirtfront, was waving at her from the banks a quarter mile upriver from where the few remaining mounted congregants still fired upon the steamboat.

He turned around, Hayes thought. He swam south rather than north toward the boat.

A half-grin was affixed to the face overcome with fatigue, his eyelids drooping. Tompal Banks turned and clambered from the silt, fading from sight into the shadow of the treeline.

Hayes hoped he made it and that whatever city or town he found would show him mercy.

The mute silently said goodbye to the man she did not know was her father, but loved just as strongly.

"You made it," Hayes said.

She staggered toward him and slid down the rail to his

side, resting her head on his shoulder.

He smelled her hair that didn't smell like a woman's should.

He didn't mind.

She would never act like his wife had and expect him to be something he was not, for she understood men like Tompal Banks, men like himself.

He would keep his promise to the man he had tried to bring to the judge's scaffold and do everything he could to help the world show the scarred Jonna mercy. For the town named after the Christian virtue, perhaps the most beautiful word Hayes could think of as he lay there bleeding, had not.

Jonathan Ashley was the author of five novels and several short stories. His work appeared in *Crime Factory*, *Out of the Gutter*, *A Twist of Noir*, *LEO Weekly*, *Kentucky Magazine* and *Yellow Mama*. The crime fiction community lost a rising star when Ashley unexpected passed away in September 2017.

On the following pages are a few
more great titles from the
Down & Out Books publishing family.

For a complete list of books and to
sign up for our newsletter,
go to DownAndOutBooks.com.

Dirty Boulevard
Crime Fiction Inspired by the Songs of Lou Reed
David James Keaton, Editor

Down & Out Books
September 2018
978-1-948235-49-5

Inspired by the outcasts, outlaws, and other outré inhabitants of rock legend Lou Reed's songbook, *Dirty Boulevard* traffics in crime fiction that's sometimes velvety and sometimes vicious, but always, absolutely, rock & roll.

Inside, you'll find stories from the fire escapes to the underground, stories filled with metal machine music, stories for gender-bending, rule-breaking, mind-blasting midnight revelries and drunken, dangerous, dark nights of the heart.

Mental State
M. Todd Henderson

Down & Out Books
October 2018
978-1-948235-33-4

How far would you go to find your brother's killer?

When law professor Alex Johnson is found dead from a gunshot wound, everyone thinks it's suicide.

Everyone except his brother, an FBI agent.

Agent Johnson goes rogue—from the ivy-covered university, to the streets of Chicago, to the halls of power in Washington. Secrets emerge that alter the course of history.

Selena
Book 1 of the Selena Series
Greg Barth

All Due Respect, an imprint of
Down & Out Books
978-1-946502-79-7

Selena is living the dream on her terms—carefree and sloppy and all in the pursuit of pleasure. When a careless act of petty theft puts her in the crosshairs of a violent crime syndicate, her choices are clear—either curl up and die, or tear down the whole damned organization one bloody shotgun blast at a time.

Nothing will satisfy her but savage retribution. Nothing can stop her. Get ready.

The Science of Paul
A Paul Little Novel of Crime
Aaron Philip Clark

Shotgun Honey, an imprint of
Down & Out Books
June 2018
978-1-948235-00-6

Ex-convict Paul Little dreams of starting a new life on a farm in North Carolina but when he gets involved with a petty thug who is later murdered, Paul is pinned between the volatile gangster accused of the crime and the straight-laced detective who sent Paul to prison years ago.

Facing danger at every turn, Paul will have to navigate Philadelphia's mean streets and match his wits with hustlers, cops, and killers.